THE ROYAL HOUSE OF KAREDES

Two crowns, two islands, one legacy

A royal family, torn apart by pride and its lust for power, reunited by purity and passion

The islands of Adamas have been torn into
two rival kingdoms:

TWO CROWNS
The Stefani diamond has been split as a
symbol of their feud

TWO ISLANDS
Gorgeous Greek princes reign supreme
over glamorous Aristo
Smouldering sheikhs rule the desert island of Calista

ONE LEGACY
Whoever reunites the diamonds will rule all.

THE ROYAL HOUSE OF KAREDES

Many years ago there were two islands ruled as one kingdom – Adamas. But bitter family feuds and rivalry caused the kingdom to be ripped in two. The islands were ruled separately, as Aristo and Calista, and the infamous Stefani coronation diamond was split as a symbol of the feud and placed in the two new crowns.

But when the king divided the islands between his son and daughter, he left them with these words:

"You will rule each island for the good of the people and bring out the best in your kingdom. But my wish is that eventually these two jewels, like the islands, will be reunited. Aristo and Calista are more successful, more beautiful and more powerful as one nation: Adamas."

Now, King Aegeus Karedes of Aristo is dead, the island's coronation diamond is missing! The Aristans will stop at nothing to get it back but the ruthless sheikh king of Calista is hot on their heels.

Whether by seduction, blackmail or marriage, the jewel must be found. As the stories unfold, secrets and sins from the past are revealed and desire, love and passion war with royal duty. But who will discover in time that it is innocence of body and purity of heart that can unite the islands of Adamas once again?

THE ROYAL
HOUSE OF KAREDES

THE SHEIKH'S FORBIDDEN VIRGIN
KATE HEWITT

Presented by

MILLS & BOON®
MODERN™

DID YOU PURCHASE THIS BOOK WITHOUT A COVER?

If you did, you should be aware it is **stolen property** as it was
reported *unsold and destroyed* by a retailer. Neither the author nor
the publisher has received any payment for this book.

All the characters in this book have no existence outside the
imagination of the author, and have no relation whatsoever to
anyone bearing the same name or names. They are not even
distantly inspired by any individual known or unknown to the
author, and all the incidents are pure invention.

All Rights Reserved including the right of reproduction in whole or
in part in any form. This edition is published by arrangement with
Harlequin Enterprises II B.V./S.à.r.l. The text of this publication or
any part thereof may not be reproduced or transmitted in any form
or by any means, electronic or mechanical, including photocopying,
recording, storage in an information retrieval system, or otherwise,
without the written permission of the publisher.

This book is sold subject to the condition that it shall not, by way of
trade or otherwise, be lent, resold, hired out or otherwise circulated
without the prior consent of the publisher in any form of binding or
cover other than that in which it is published and without a similar
condition including this condition being imposed on the subsequent
purchaser.

® and ™ are trademarks owned and used by the trademark owner
and/or its licensee. Trademarks marked with ® are registered
with the United Kingdom Patent Office and/or the Office for
Harmonisation in the Internal Market and in other countries.

First published in Great Britain 2009
by Harlequin Mills & Boon Limited,
Eton House, 18-24 Paradise Road, Richmond, Surrey TW9 1SR

The Sheikh's Forbidden Virgin © Harlequin Books S.A. 2009

Special thanks and acknowledgement are given to Kate Hewitt
for her contribution to *The Royal House of Karedes* series

ISBN: 978 0 263 87554 6

53-0809

Printed and bound in Spain
by Litografía Rosés S.A., Barcelona

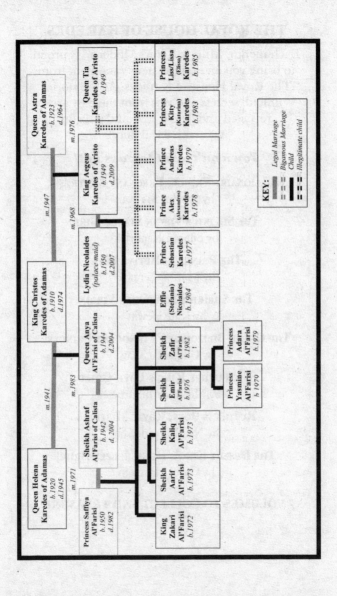

THE ROYAL HOUSE OF KAREDES

THE ROYAL HOUSE OF KAREDES

Each month, Mills & Boon® Modern™ is proud
to bring you an exciting new instalment from
The Royal House of Karedes. As the stories
unfold, secrets and sins from the past are
revealed and desire, love and passion
war with royal duty!

You won't want to miss out!

BILLIONAIRE PRINCE, PREGNANT MISTRESS
by Sandra Marton

THE SHEIKH'S VIRGIN STABLE-GIRL
by Sharon Kendrick

THE PRINCE'S CAPTIVE WIFE
by Marion Lennox

THE SHEIKH'S FORBIDDEN VIRGIN
by Kate Hewitt

THE GREEK BILLIONAIRE'S INNOCENT PRINCESS
by Chantelle Shaw

THE FUTURE KING'S LOVE-CHILD
by Melanie Milburne

RUTHLESS BOSS, ROYAL MISTRESS
by Natalie Anderson

THE DESERT KING'S HOUSEKEEPER BRIDE
by Carol Marinelli

8 VOLUMES TO COLLECT AND TREASURE!

CHAPTER ONE

THE dream came to him again. It was an assault of the senses and of memory, a tangle of images, grasping hands, the choking sea. Aarif Al'Farisi slept with his eyes clenched shut, his hands fisted on his bed sheets, a sheen of sweat glistening on his skin.

'Help me…help me…Aarif!'

The desperate cry of his name echoed endlessly, helplessly through the corridors of time and memory.

Aarif woke suddenly; his eyes opened and adjusted to the darkness of his bedroom. A pale sliver of moon cast a jagged swathe of light on the floor. He took a deep, shuddering breath and sat up, swinging his legs over the side of the bed.

It took a moment to calm his racing heart. Each careful, measured breath steadied him and made the shadows retreat. For now. He ran a hand through his sleep-tousled hair, still damp with sweat, and rose from the bed.

From the balcony of the Calistan royal palace he could see an endless stretch of moonlit sand, arid desert, all the way to the Kordela river with its diamonds, Calista's lifeblood, mixed treacherously in its silt. He kept his gaze on the undulating waves of sand and the promise of the river with its guarded treasure, and let his breathing return to normal as a dry desert wind cooled the sweat on his skin.

He hated his dreams. He hated that even now, twenty years later, they left him shaken, afraid, helpless. Weak. Instinctively Aarif shook his head, as if to deny the dream. The reality. For the truth, stark as it was, was that he'd failed his brother and his family all those years ago, and he was destined to relive those agonising moments in his mind whenever the dreams visited him.

He hadn't had a dream like this for months, and the respite had lulled him into a false sense of security. Safety. Yet he would never have either, he knew. How could you be safe from yourself, secure from the endless repercussions of your own failures?

Letting out a sigh of frustrated exasperation, Aarif turned from the balcony and the inky night spangled with stars. He moved to the laptop he'd left on the desk by his bed, for he knew sleep was far off now. He would redeem the night through work.

He opened the computer and the machine

hummed to life as he pulled on a pair of loose-fitting cotton trousers, his chest and feet still bare. In the mirror above the bureau he caught a glimpse of his reflection, saw the remembered fear still etched in harsh lines on his face, flared in his eyes, and he grimaced in self-disgust.

Afraid, after all these years. Still. He shook his head again, and turned to the computer. He checked his e-mail first; there were several clients he had appointments with in the next week who needed careful handling. Calista's diamonds were precious, but the island did not possess the vast reserves of Africa or Australia, and clients needed to be counted—and treated—carefully.

Yet there were no e-mails from clients in his message inbox, he saw, just one from his brother, King Zakari of Calista. Aarif's brows snapped together as he read his brother's instructions.

I must follow a lead on the diamond. Go to Zaraq and fetch Kalila. Ever your brother, Zakari.

The diamond...the Stefani diamond, the jewel of the Adamas Crown, split in two when the islands' rule had been divided. Aarif had never seen the diamond in its unified whole of course; the Calistan crown held only half of the gem. The other half, meant to be in the Aristan crown, was missing, and proving to be utterly elusive. By tradition, uniting the diamond was believed to be the key to uniting the kingdoms of Aristo and Calista for ever. Aarif had seen how determined Zakari was to retrieve that precious stone, and with it gain a kingdom.

So determined, in fact, that he now delegated this new responsibility to Aarif. Zakari's e-mail message contained a simple directive, yet one fraught with decisions, details, and potential disaster. For Princess Kalila Zadar was Zakari's betrothed and their wedding was in a fortnight.

The retrieval of a royal bride was a complex and cautious affair, one that rested on ceremony, courtesy, and tradition. Aarif knew he would have to play his hand—and his brother's hand—very carefully so as not to offend Kalila, her father King Bahir, or the people of Zaraq. The alliance with Zaraq was important and influential, and could not be treated lightly.

Aarif pressed his lips together in a hard line before touching his fingers to the computer keys. His reply was simple: *I will do as you instruct. Your servant, Aarif.*

There was never any possibility of questioning Zakari, or refusing his brother's demand. Aarif did not even consider it for a moment. His sense of obedience and responsibility were absolute; his family and kingdom came first. Always.

Aarif glanced up from the screen. Dawn was beginning to streak across the sky, pale fingers of light that illuminated the mist-shrouded dunes below. In that eerie grey half-light Aarif caught another glimpse of his face in the mirror, and for a moment he was startled by his own reflection, still surprised even now by the puckered finger of scar tissue that ran from his brow to his jaw, for ever a reminder of how he'd once failed in his duty to his family and kingdom.

He would never do so again.

Kalila woke from a restless sleep as the sun slanted through the window of her bedroom in the Zaraquan palace, the gauzy curtains stirring lazily in the hot breeze.

Nerves jumped and writhed in her belly, and one hand stole to her middle and rested there, as if she could calm the thoughts and fears that raced through her.

Today she would meet her husband.

She swung her feet over the side of the bed and padded barefoot to the window. The sky was already hard and bright, an endless stretch of blue without a single cloud. Beneath the sky the desert rolled away to the sea, little more than a pale blue-green shimmering on the horizon, marked by the slim stretch of verdant fields by the water's edge. The rest of Zaraq, a small kingdom, was desert. Dry, barren, and unproductive save for a few copper and nickel mines that now provided nearly all of the country's revenue.

Kalila swallowed. And that, she reminded

herself, was the reason she was marrying at all. Zaraq needed Calista. Her father needed the security of Calista's diamond mines, and Calista needed Zaraq's stability of over a hundred years of uninterrupted independent rule. It was simple, depressingly so. She was a pawn, a bargaining chip, and she'd always known it.

Kalila rested her forehead against the mellow, golden stone of the window frame, still cool with the memory of night, although the sun slanting onto her skin was hot.

What would Zakari look like after all these years? What would he think of her? She knew he wouldn't love her. He hadn't seen her since she was a child, skinny and awkward, with too much hair and a gap-toothed smile. She barely remembered him; her mind played with shadowed memories of someone tall, powerful, commanding. Charismatic. He'd smiled at her, patted her head, and that was all.

Until now…when the stranger would become the bridegroom.

Today she would see him at last, and would he be pleased with his intended spouse? Would she?

A light, perfunctory knock sounded on the door and then her childhood nurse, Juhanah, bustled into the room.

'Good! You are awake. I've brought you breakfast, and then we must ready your beautiful self.

His reverence could be here by noon, or so I've been told. We have much to do.'

Kalila suppressed a sigh as she turned from the window. Her father had told her yesterday just what kind of reception Sheikh Zakari must have.

'He must see a traditional girl, well brought up and fit to be a royal bride. You need not speak or even look at him, it would be too bold,' King Bahir warned, softening his words with a smile, although his eyes were still stern. 'You understand, Kalila? Tomorrow's meeting with Sheikh Zakari is important, and it is crucial that you present the right image. Juhanah will help you with the preparations.'

Not even speak? Every Western sensibility Kalila had ever possessed rose and rankled. 'Why can't Sheikh Zakari see me as I am?' she protested, trying to keep a petulant note from entering her voice. She was twenty-four years old, a university educated woman, about to be married, yet in her father's presence she still felt like an unruly child. She moderated her tone, striving for an answering smile. 'Surely, Father, it is just as important that he knows who his bride really is. If we present the wrong impression—'

'I know what the wrong impression is,' Bahir cut her off, his tone ominously final. 'And also what the right one is. There is time for him to *know* you, as you so wish, later,' he added, and Kalila flinched at the blatant dismissal of her desire. Bahir lifted one hand as though he were bestowing a blessing, although it felt more like a warning, a scolding. 'Tomorrow is not about you, Kalila. It is not even about your marriage. It is about tradition and ceremony, an alliance of countries, families. It has always been this way.'

Kalila's eyes flashed. 'Even for my mother?'

Bahir's lips compressed. 'Yes, even for her. Your mother was modern, Kalila, but she was not stubborn.' He sighed. 'I gave you your years at Cambridge, your university degree. You have pursued your interests and had your turn. Now it is your family's turn, your country's turn, and after all this waiting, you must do your duty. It begins tomorrow.' Despite the glimmer of compassion in his eyes, he spoke flatly, finally, and Kalila straightened, throwing her shoulders back with proud defiance.

'I know it well, Father.' Yet she couldn't help but take note of his words. Pursue her interests, he'd said, but not her dreams. And what good were interests if they had to be laid down for the sake of duty? And what *were* her dreams?

Her mind wrapped itself seductively around the question, the possibility. Her dreams were shadowy, shapeless things, visions of joy, happiness, meaning and purpose. Love. The word slipped unbidden in her mind, a seed planted in the fertile soil of her imagination, already taking root.

Love…but there was no love involved in this union between two strangers. There was not even affection, and Kalila had no idea if there ever would be. Could Zakari love her? Would he? And, Kalila wondered now as Juhanah bustled around her bedroom, would she love him?

Could she?

'Now eat.' Juhanah prodded her towards the tray set with a bowl of *labneh*, thick, creamy yoghurt, and a cup of strong, sweet coffee. 'You need your strength. We have much to do today.'

Kalila sat down at the table and took a bite. 'Just what *are* we doing today, Juhanah?'

Juhanah's chest swelled and she puffed out her already round cheeks. 'Your father wants you to be prepared as a girl was in the old days, when tradition mattered.' She frowned, and Kalila knew her nurse was thinking of her Western ways, inherited from her English mother and firmly rooted after four years of independent living in Cambridge.

When Kalila had discarded a pair of jeans on the floor of her bedroom Juhanah had pinched the offending garment between two plump fingers and held it away from her as if it were contaminated. Kalila grinned ruefully in memory.

'His Eminence will want to see you as a proper bride,' Juhanah said now, parroting her father's words from yesterday.

Kalila smiled, mischief glinting in her eyes. 'When shall I call him Zakari, do you think?'

'When he is in your bed,' Juhanah replied with an uncharacteristic frankness. 'Do not be too bold beforehand, my love. Men don't like a forward girl.'

'Oh, Juhanah!' Kalila shook her head. 'You've never left Zaraq, you don't know what it's like out there. Zakari has been to university, he's a man of the world—' So she had read in the newspapers and tabloid magazines. So she *hoped*.

'Pfft.' Juhanah blew out her cheeks once more. 'And so, do I need to know such things? What matters is here and now, my princess. King Zakari will want to see a royal princess today, not a modern girl with her fancy degree.' This was said with rolled eyes; Kalila knew Juhanah thought very little of her years in England. And in truth, she reflected, sitting at the table with the breakfast tray before her, those years counted for very little now.

What counted was her pedigree, her breeding, her body. Zakari wanted an alliance, not an ally. He wasn't looking for a lover, a partner. A soulmate.

Kalila's mouth twisted in bitter acknowledgement. She knew all this; she'd reminded herself of it fiercely every day that she'd been waiting for her wedding, her husband. Yet now the waiting was over, she found her heart was anxious for more.

'Aren't you hungry, *ya daanaya*?' Juhanah

pressed, prodding the bowl of *labneh* as if she could induce Kalila to take a bit.

Kalila shook her head and pushed the bowl away. Her nerves, jumping and leaping, writhing and roiling, had returned, and she knew she would not manage another bite. 'I'll just have coffee,' she said, smiling to appease her nurse, and took a sip of the thick, sweet liquid. It scalded her tongue and burned down to her belly, with the same fierce resolve that fired her heart.

The bridal preparations took all morning. Kalila had expected it, and of course she wanted to look her best. Yet amidst all the ministrations, the lotions and creams and paints and powders, she couldn't help but feel like a chicken being trussed and seasoned for the cooking pot.

There was only Juhanah and a kitchen maid to act as her *negaffa*, the women who prepared the bride; the Zaraquan palace had a small staff since her mother had died.

First, she had a milk bath in the women's bathing quarters, an ancient tradition that Kalila wasn't sure she liked. Supposedly the milk of goats was good for the skin, yet it also had a peculiar smell.

'I wouldn't mind a bit of bath foam from the chemists',' she muttered, not loud enough for Juhanah or the kitchen maid to hear. They wouldn't understand, anyway.

As Juhanah towelled her dry and rubbed sweet-smelling lotion into her skin Kalila felt a sudden pang of sorrow and grief for her mother, who had died when Kalila had been only seventeen. Her mother Amelia had been English, cool and lovely, and it would have been her loving duty to prepare Kalila for this meeting with her bridegroom.

She, Kalila acknowledged with a rueful sorrow, would have understood about bath foam. They could have teased, laughed, enjoyed themselves even with the pall of duty hanging over her, the knowledge of what was to come.

Still, she reminded herself, she could be modern later. She could be *herself* later, when she and Zakari were alone. The thought of such an occurrence turned her mouth dry and set her nerves leaping once more.

Yet they would not be alone today. Today was for the formal meeting of a royal king and his bride, a piece of theatre elaborately staged and played, and she was merely a prop…one of many.

'No frowns,' Juhanah chided her gently. 'Only smiles today, my princess!'

Kalila forced a smile but she felt a pall of gloom settle over her like a shroud. The future loomed dark and unknowable ahead of her, a twisting road with an uncertain destination.

She hadn't seen or spoken to Zakari since she was little more than a child. There had been letters, birthday presents, polite and impersonal inquiries. Tradition demanded there be no more, and yet today she would meet him. In two weeks she would marry him.

It was absurd, archaic, and yet it was her life. The rest of it, anyway. Kalila swallowed the acidic taste of fear.

'Look.' Juhanah steered her towards the mirror, and even after the hours of preparation Kalila wasn't expecting the change. She looked…like a stranger.

The red and gold kaftan swallowed her slight figure, and her hair had been twisted back into an elaborate plait. Heavy gold jewellery settled at her wrists and throat, and her face…

Kalila didn't recognise the full red lips, or the wide, dark eyes outlined in kohl. She looked exotic, unfamiliar. Ridiculous, she thought with a sudden surge of bitterness. Like a male fantasy come to life.

'Beautiful, yes?' Juhanah said happily, and the kitchen maid nodded in agreement. Kalila could only stare. 'And now, the final touch…' Juhanah slipped the veil over her head, the garment of feminine pride, the hijab. It covered her hair and a diaphanous veil spangled with gold and silver coins covered her face, leaving nothing but those wide, blank, kohl-lined eyes. 'There,' Juhanah sighed in satisfaction.

Gazing at her exotic reflection, it seemed impossible that only eight months ago she'd been in Cambridge, debating philosophy and eating pizza with friends on the floor of her student flat. Wearing jeans, completely unchaperoned, living a life of freedom and opportunity, intellectual pursuit and joy.

Joy. She felt utterly joyless now, standing, staring there, utterly alien. Who was she? Was she the girl in Cambridge, laughing and flirting and talking politics, or was she this girl in the mirror, with her dark eyes and hidden face?

Eight months ago her father had come to England, taken her out for a meal and listened to her girlish chatter. She'd thought—deceived herself—that he was merely visiting her. That he *missed* her. Of course there had been a greater plan, a deeper need. There always had been.

Kalila still remembered the moment she'd seen her father's face turn sombre, one hand coming to rest lightly on hers so the spill of silly talk died on her lips, and her mouth went dry. 'What…?' she'd whispered, yet she'd known. Of course she'd known. She'd always known, since she had been twelve, when she'd had her engagement party.

She and Zakari had exchanged rings, although she barely remembered the ceremony. It was a blur of images and sensations, the cloying scent of jasmine, the heavy weight of the ring, a Calistan diamond, that Zakari had slipped on her finger. It had been far too big, and she'd put it in her jewellery box, where it had remained ever since.

Perhaps, Kalila thought distantly, she should wear it again.

'I know the wedding has been put off many times,' Bahir said, his voice surprisingly gentle. It made Kalila's eyes sting, and she stared down at her plate. 'Family obligations on both sides have made it so. But finally King Zakari is ready to wed. He has set a date…May the twenty-fifth.'

Kalila swallowed. It was the end of September, the leaves just starting to turn gold, flooding the Cambridge backs with colour, and the start of her term. 'But…' she began, and Bahir shook his head.

'Kalila, we always knew this was your destiny. Your duty. I have already spoken to the registrar. Your course has been cancelled.'

She jerked her head up, her eyes meeting his, seeing the implacable insistence there. 'You had no right—'

'I had every right,' Bahir replied, and now she heard the hard implacability, felt it. 'I am your father and your king. You have received your degree—the post-graduate course was merely a way to pass the time.'

Kalila swallowed. Her throat ached so much the instinctive movement hurt. 'It was more than that to me,' she whispered.

'Yes, perhaps,' Bahir allowed, his shoulders

moving in a tiny shrug, 'but you always knew what the future held. Your mother and I never kept it from you.'

No, they hadn't. They'd spoken to her before that wretched party, explained what it meant to be a princess, the joy that lay in fulfilling one's duty. Propaganda, and Kalila had believed it with all her childish heart. She'd been dazzled by the crown prince of Calista, although now she didn't remember much of Zakari, no more than a tall, charismatic presence, a patient—or had it been patronising?—smile. She'd only been twelve, after all.

'You will come home with me,' Bahir finished, beckoning to the waiter to clear their plates. 'You have a day to say goodbye to your friends and pack what you need.'

'A day?' Kalila repeated in disbelief. Her life was being dismantled in an instant, as if it had been meaningless, trivial—

And to her father, it had.

'I want you home,' Bahir said. 'Where you belong.'

'But if I'm not getting married until May—'

'Your presence is needed in your country, Kalila.' Bahir's voice turned stern; she'd worn his patience too thin with her desperate, fruitless resistance. 'Your people need to see you. You have been away nearly four years. It is time to come home.'

That evening, packing up her paltry possessions, Kalila had considered the impossible. The unthinkable. She could defy her father, run away from her so-called destiny. Stay in Cambridge, live her own life, find her own husband or lover…

Yet even as these thoughts, desperate and treacherous, flitted through her mind, she discarded them. Where could she run? With what money? And what would she do?

Besides, she acknowledged starkly, too much of her life—her blood—was bound up in this country, this world. Zaraq's future was bound with Calista's; to risk her country's well-being for her own selfish, feminine desires was contemptible. She could never betray her father, her country in such a manner. It would be a betrayal of herself.

So she'd returned home with her father on his private plane, had settled back into life in the empty palace with its skeleton staff. She drifted from day to day, room to room, at first trying to keep up with her studies in history and then discarding them in depression.

She'd attended to her civic responsibilities, visiting sick children, new businesses, shaking hands and cutting ribbons, smiling and nodding. She enjoyed the interactions with the people of Zaraq, but at times it felt like only so much busy work, a lifetime of busy work, for that was her duty.

Her destiny.

Now, gazing into the mirror, she wished—even wondered if—her destiny lay elsewhere. Surely she'd been made for, meant to do, more than this. Be more than this.

'Princess?' Juhanah said softly. 'Beautiful, *n'am*?'

Kalila had a desperate, intense urge to rip the veil from her face. She'd never been veiled before—her mother had refused, wearing only Western clothes, her nod to old-fashioned propriety no more than a scrap of head covering on formal occasions. Her father hadn't minded. He'd married his English rose as part of an attempt to Westernise his country. Yet now, Kalila thought with renewed bitterness, she looked like something out of the *Arabian Nights*. Like a harem girl. The coins tinkled when she moved.

'Lovely,' Juhanah murmured. Kalila's fingers bunched on the gauzy material of her kaftan and a fingernail snagged on a bit of gold thread.

Juhanah tutted and batted her hand away. Just then a knock sounded on the door of the bedroom, and Juhanah went to answer it while Kalila continued to stare.

What would Zakari think of her like this? Was this what he wanted? Was this what her future looked like?

She swallowed, forcing the fears and doubts back. It was too late now, far too late. She understood her duty.

She just hadn't known how it would *feel*.

Juhanah padded back into the bedroom and flitted around Kalila, tugging a bit of material here, smoothing it there. 'You are radiant,' she said and beneath the veil Kalila's lips twisted sardonically. Was Juhanah blind, or just blinded by her own happiness? Her nurse was thrilled Kalila was fulfilling her duty and destiny as a crown princess. A queen. 'And it is time,' she continued, her eyes lighting, her plump cheeks flushed with excitement. 'The sheikh has just arrived. He's coming directly from the plane.' And as if she didn't understand already, her heart already beginning to hammer a frantic, desperate beat, Juhanah added in satisfaction, 'Finally, he is here.'

Aarif was hot, dusty, and tired. The short ride in an open Jeep from the royal airstrip to the palace itself was enough to nearly cover him in dust. He'd been met by a palace official who would take him to the palace's throne room, where he would extend Zakari's formal greetings to his bride and her father.

Aarif swallowed and the dust caught grittily in his throat and stung his eyes. Already he'd seen the official sweep a cautious gaze over his face, linger on that damnable line from forehead to jaw. His scar. His reminder, and everyone else's, of his flaws, his failures.

The palace emerged in the distance, long and

low, of mellow golden stone, with towers on either end. In every other direction the desert stretched to an empty horizon, although Aarif thought he glimpsed a huddle of clay and stone buildings to the west—Makaris, the nation's capital.

The Jeep pulled up to the front entrance, a pair of intricately carved wooden doors under a stone canopy.

'I will take you to wash and prepare yourself, Your Highness,' the official said, bowing. 'King Bahir awaits you in the throne room.'

Aarif nodded, and followed the man into the palace, down a cool, stone corridor and to a waiting chamber with benches and a table. There was a pitcher of lemon water, and Aarif poured a glass and drank thirstily before he changed into his *bisht*, the long, formal robe worn for ceremonies such as this. In the adjoining bathroom he washed the dust from his face, his eyes sliding away from his reflection in the mirror before returning resolutely to stare at his face, as he always did.

A light, inquiring knock sounded on the door, and, turning from that grim reminder, Aarif left the bathroom and went to fulfil his brother's bidding, and express his greetings to his bride.

The official led him to the double doors of the throne room; inside an expectant hush fell like a curtain being dropped into place, or perhaps pulled up.

'Your Eminence,' the official said in French, the national language of Zaraq, his voice low and unctuous, 'may I present His Royal Highness, King Zakari.'

Aarif choked; the sound was lost amidst a ripple of murmurings from the palace staff that had assembled for this honoured occasion. It would only take King Bahir one glance to realise it was not the king who graced his throne room today, but rather the king's brother, a lowly prince.

Aarif felt a flash of rage—directed at himself. A mistake had been made in the correspondence, he supposed. He'd delegated the task to an aide when he should have written himself and explained that he would be coming rather than his brother.

Now he would have to explain the mishap in front of company, all of Bahir's staff, and he feared the insult could be great.

'Your Eminence,' he said, also speaking French, and moved into the long, narrow room with its frescoed ceilings and bare walls. He bowed, not out of obeisance but rather respect, and heard Bahir shift in his chair. 'I fear my brother, His Royal Highness Zakari, was unable to attend to this glad errand, due to pressing royal business. I am honoured to escort his bride, the Princess Kalila, to Calista in his stead.'

Bahir was silent, and, stifling a prickle of both alarm and irritation, Aarif rose. He was conscious of Bahir watching him, his skin smooth but his eyes shrewd, his mouth tightening with disappointment or displeasure, perhaps both.

Yet even before Bahir made a reply, even before the formalities had been dispensed with, Aarif found his gaze sliding, of its own accord, to the silent figure to Bahir's right.

It was his daughter, of course. Kalila. Aarif had a memory of a pretty, precocious child. He'd spoken a few words to her at the engagement party more than ten years ago now. Yet now the woman standing before him was lovely, although, he acknowledged wryly, he could see little of her.

Her head was bowed, her figure swathed in a kaftan, and yet as if she felt the magnetic tug of his gaze she lifted her head, and her eyes met his.

It was all he could see of her, those eyes; they were almond-shaped, wide and dark, luxuriously fringed, a deep, clear golden brown. Every emotion could be seen in them, including the one that flickered there now as her gaze was drawn inexorably to his face, to his scar.

It was disgust Aarif thought he saw flare in their golden depths and as their gazes held and clashed he felt a sharp, answering stab of disappointment and self-loathing in his own gut.

CHAPTER TWO

HE HADN'T come. Kalila gazed blankly at the stranger in front of her, heard the words, the explanations, the expected flattery, the apologies and regrets, but none of it made sense.

She couldn't get her head—her heart—around the fact that her husband-to-be hadn't bothered to show up. Would he even be at the wedding? Hadn't he realised she'd been waiting, wondering, hoping…?

Or had he even bothered to think about her at all?

She swallowed the bubble of hysterial laughter that threatened to rise up and spill out. Her father was speaking, his voice low and melodious, inviting this man—who was he? Kalila's brain scrambled for the remembered words, fragments—Prince Aarif. Zakari's younger brother, sent on this *glad errand*. Her lips twisted cynically, but of course no one could see her smile behind this damned veil.

Her fingers clenched at her side. She longed to rip off the veil, destroy the entire charade, because that was all it was. A charade, a façade. False.

A piece of theatre, and she no longer wanted the role.

She wanted to run, to run and never stop until she was somewhere safe and different, somewhere she could be herself—whoever that was—and people would be glad.

Where, she wondered hopelessly, was that place? She didn't think she had found it yet.

Her father had risen, and Kalila knew this was her cue to gracefully withdraw. This pretty little part had been scripted, rehearsed. She bowed, lowering her head with its heavy plait and awkward veil, and backed slowly out of the room, trying not to trip over the embroidered hem of her kaftan. She couldn't wait to get out of this get-up, to be *free*.

She tore the veil from her face as soon as she was out of the room, grabbing a fistful of the kaftan to clear her feet as she strode to her bedroom. Juhanah followed, tutting anxiously.

'The fabric—it is delicate!' she protested, reaching for the veil Kalila had fisted in one hand.

'I don't care,' she snapped, and Juhanah clucked again, prising the veil from Kalila's fingers and smoothing it carefully.

'You are disappointed, of course. But the king

is a busy man, with many demands. It is just as well you become accustomed to this early, *ya daanaya*.'

'Even before we've met?' Kalila heard the sarcastic edge to her voice and was glad. She needed to vent her feelings, her frustration, for Juhanah was right, she was disappointed. Disappointed and hurt.

And she had no reason to be, because she had never thought Zakari loved her. How could he? So what had she been hoping for? She didn't know, couldn't answer, yet she felt deep in her belly, her soul, that something had been irretrievably lost today. She just didn't know what it was.

Back in the sanctuary of her bedroom she took a deep, steadying breath. She knew there was no point in acting like a petulant child; she was a woman, with a woman's life ahead of her. A woman's duty, a woman's burden.

Her mind slid back to the night eight months ago, alone in her Cambridge flat, when she could have walked away. She could have cut herself off from her father, her family, her country and culture. A small part of her would have welcomed it.

Yet she hadn't, and she knew in her heart she never would have. Despite the endless, aching uncertainty and regret, she had a duty to her family. To herself.

And yet. And yet she hadn't expected this. This hurt, this disappointment, so fresh and raw and painful.

She had been nourishing dreams without even

realising it. Those shadowy dreams took form now as she acknowledged her own folly. She'd wanted Zakari to come here, to be eager for this day, and then to be speechless at the sight of her. She'd wanted him to be enchanted, enamoured, in love.

And all without even knowing her! She really was a fool. A child, to believe in such childish dreams, such fairy tales. To have let herself hope even when she thought she was being realistic, responsible. She'd fooled *herself*.

Kalila sighed wearily as she stared at her painted face in the mirror. A fan whirred lazily above her but the heat of midday was oppressive, made even more so by her heavy garments.

'Please help me, Juhanah,' she said. She pulled at the kaftan. 'I want to get this off.'

'Of course, of course,' Juhanah soothed, hurrying to her side. 'You will want to rest, to be fresh for this evening.'

Kalila frowned. 'Why? What's happening this evening?'

'Did you not hear? Your father invited Prince Aarif to dine with you both tonight. Informal, he said.' Juhanah's smile glinted knowingly. 'No kaftan, no hijab.'

Kalila breathed a sigh of relief as she pushed the heavy mass of hair away from her neck. 'Good.'

Juhanah slipped the kaftan from Kalila's shoulders. 'You know this was your mother's?'

'It was?' She turned in disbelief. 'I never saw her wear anything like it.'

'No, she didn't, not very often.' Juhanah ran one finger along the gold thread. 'But she wore this to her own engagement party—your father chose it as a wedding gift. She looked very beautiful.'

Kalila tried to imagine her mother, tall, slender, blonde, wearing the outfit she had. Weighed down by its heaviness and expectations. She wondered how her mother had felt wearing it. Had she been as stifled and suppressed as Kalila had? Or had she seen it only as a costume, and a beautiful one at that?

Her mother had chosen to marry Bahir, she knew. It had been, against all odds, a love match.

So why, Kalila wondered as Juhanah quietly left the room and she stretched out restlessly on her bed, couldn't she have the same?

Surprisingly, she slept, although she'd felt too anxious and upset to even close her eyes at first. Somehow she fell into an uneasy sleep, where even her dreams were tinted with a vague unhappiness.

When she awoke, the sun was low in the sky, and the breeze blowing in from the window was blessedly cool.

Kalila pushed her hair away from her eyes and moved to the window. The sun was a fiery ball of orange, sending vivid streaks of light across a sky just darkening to dusk. It was a stark yet beautiful sight, and one she never tired of. She'd missed sunsets like these in England. She'd missed the purity of light and air, the violent brightness of the colours.

A glance at the clock told her she needed to ready herself quickly. The woman Prince Aarif saw tonight would be nothing like the vision of traditional womanhood he'd seen this afternoon, Kalila would make sure of that. The time for pageantry and play-acting was over. And besides, she reminded herself as she stepped into a scalding shower, there was no one to impress. Zakari wasn't even here.

She scrubbed away the kohl and the red lipstick, the scents of jasmine and sandalwood. She scrubbed until her face was clean and bare and her skin smelled only of soap.

She dressed in a simple cocktail dress, modest by Western standards, although glaringly different from her earlier outfit. It was a simple silk sheath in pale lavender, skimming her body and ending mid-calf. She slipped on a pair of matching pumps and pulled her hair up into a quick and careless chignon. The only nod to make-up was a bit of lip gloss.

Taking a deep breath, wondering just why nerves had started their restless fluttering once more, Kalila headed downstairs.

Prince Aarif was already in the palace's smaller, less formal dining room, drink in hand, when she arrived. Kalila paused on the threshold, taking in the table set intimately for three, and then the prince standing by the window, his back half to her. Her father was nowhere in sight.

She hadn't given their unexpected guest more than a passing thought since she'd seen him that afternoon; it had been Zakari's absence that had occupied her thoughts rather than Aarif's presence.

Yet now she found her gaze resting on him, sweeping over him in open curiosity. He wore a Western suit in charcoal grey and it fitted his long, lithe form with gracious ease. He looked so different in these clothes than in his *bisht*, Kalila realised, so much more approachable and human. She wondered if she did as well.

Then, as if he sensed her presence, he turned to face her fully, and Kalila drew in a breath at the sight of his face, his eyes curiously blank although his lips were curved in a smile of greeting, the scar curving along his cheek. He looked formal, forbidding, almost angry even though he smiled.

Kalila forced herself to smile back. 'Good evening, Prince Aarif.'

Aarif nodded once. 'Princess.'

She stepped into the room, strangely conscious of the fact that they were alone, although even that was a fantasy. Servants were within earshot and her father would undoubtedly arrive in a few minutes. 'Did you have a good afternoon?' she asked, and heard the bright falsity in her own voice.

Aarif's mouth flickered in something not quite a smile. 'An enlightening one,' he replied, and took a sip of his drink. He gestured to her own empty hand. 'Would you like a drink?'

As if on cue, a servant came forward and Kalila asked for a glass of fruit juice. She wanted to keep her head clear.

'I'm afraid I don't remember you,' Kalila said, smiling ruefully. 'You must be Zakari's younger brother, but I know he has many, and sisters too…'

'Yes, there are seven of us.' Aarif's hard gaze settled on her as he added, 'I remember you. You were quite young at that engagement party, weren't you? You wore a white dress, with a bow in your hair.'

'I was twelve,' Kalila replied, her voice coming out in almost a whisper before she cleared her throat. She was touched—and unsettled—that he remembered her dress, her hair.

'You looked as if you were going to a birthday party.' Aarif glanced away. 'Perhaps it felt like that at the time.'

Kalila nodded, surprised and unsettled again that he could understand just how she'd felt. 'Yes, it did. And I was getting the best present of all.' The trace of bitterness in her voice must have alerted him, for he glanced at her with faint censure now, the moment of unexpected closeness shattered by her own confession.

'Marriage is an honour and a blessing.'

He sounded so much like her father, Kalila thought. Like every man who lectured about a woman's duty. 'Are you married, Prince Aarif?' she asked, a note of challenge in her voice.

Aarif shook his head. 'No,' he said flatly, and any further discussion was put to an end by the arrival of her father.

'Ah, Prince Aarif. And Kalila, you look well rested. I am glad.' He came forward, rubbing his hands together, every inch the beneficent ruler. 'I was telling Prince Aarif earlier that we do not rest on formality here, especially among family and friends.'

Then what, Kalila wanted to ask, was the point of that spectacle today? Of course she knew: tradition, ceremony. Pride. She saw her father's gaze move speculatively between her and Aarif and instinctively she took a step away from the prince. A new, hidden meaning to her father's words making her uncomfortably aware of the potential impropriety of their brief conversation. 'Yes, of course,' she said with a perfunctory smile. 'We are very glad to welcome you to Zaraq, Prince Aarif.'

'And I am very glad to be here,' he returned, his voice low, pleasant and smooth, yet somehow devoid of any true expression. Kalila glanced at his face and saw his eyes looked blank. He was wearing a mask, she thought, a veil, as much of one as she had worn this afternoon. She wondered what he was trying to hide.

Bahir drew Kalila's chair, before sitting down, and Aarif followed.

'Earlier Aarif was explaining to me why King Zakari could not be here today,' Bahir said as he poured them all wine. Kalila took a sip; it was light and refreshing and bubbled pleasantly through her.

'Oh, yes?' she said, raising her eyebrows.

'He is, of course, a busy man,' Bahir continued. 'With many royal duties. He is not, in fact, on Calista at the moment…' He let his voice trail off in delicate inquiry, and Kalila watched with a flicker of interest as Aarif's mouth tightened.

'He is not?' she asked. 'Where is he, Prince Aarif?'

'Please, call me Aarif.' There was a thread of tension in his voice that Kalila heard with growing curiosity.

'Then you must call me Kalila,' she returned as a matter of courtesy, yet this pleasantry caused Aarif's sharp gaze to rest briefly on her face and something unfurled deep in her belly and spiralled strangely upwards.

He wasn't, she reflected, taking another sip of wine, a classically handsome man. The scar put paid to that, but even without it his face was too harsh, too hard. There was no kindness in it, no humour or sympathy. The only emotion she saw in his dark eyes, in the flat line of his mouth, was determination.

She wondered just what Aarif was determined to do.

The first course, stewed chicken seasoned with coriander and paprika, was served, and they all began to eat.

'I have heard,' Bahir said after a moment, his voice mild and easy, 'rumours of diamonds.'

Aarif paused for only a fraction of a second before he smiled and shrugged. 'There are always rumours.'

'This rumour,' Bahir continued, his voice turning hard for only a second, 'is that half of the Stefani diamond is missing.' He paused, and Kalila watched as Aarif continued chewing with what looked like deliberate unconcern. 'I wonder if that is what concerns your brother, Aarif?'

Aarif swallowed and took a sip of wine. Tension crackled in the air and Kalila's gaze flickered from one man to the other, both smiling and genial, yet too much shrewd knowledge in their eyes.

What was going on?

'My brother is indeed concerned about the Stefani diamond,' Aarif said after a moment. 'It has long been his desire to unite the diamond, and of course the kingdoms of Calista and Aristo.' His gaze rested once more on Kalila, and again she felt that strange unfurling, as if inside her something had taken root and now sought sunlight, life and air. 'This, of course, is of benefit to you, Princess.

You shall be Queen not only of Calista, but of Aristo also.'

Kalila tried to smile, although in truth she hadn't considered herself queen of anything at all. She'd only been thinking of herself as someone's wife, not queen of a country, or even two.

Queen. She tried to feel the obligatory thrill, but disappointment and fear were too pressing. She didn't aspire to titles; she aspired to love.

'I wish your brother every success,' she finally said, keeping her voice light, and a servant came to clear their plates.

'My brother will be successful,' Aarif said, smiling, although there was an odd flatness to his voice, his eyes. 'When one is determined, one is also successful.'

There was a tiny pause, and the servant came to clear the dishes. 'Indeed, an excellent maxim to live by,' Bahir said lightly, and poured more wine.

Kalila toyed with the next course, a salad made with couscous, cucumbers, and tomatoes. Her appetite had vanished and she felt unsettled again, uneasy even though she was in comfortable clothes. Even though she was herself.

She didn't know what caused this sense of unease, a needy sort of dissatisfaction. Was it Zakari's absence or Aarif's presence? Her gaze flitted to the prince's hard profile, lingered briefly on the strong curve of his jaw, the livid line of his scar, and she felt again that strange spiralling within, upwards, something happy and hungry. He interested her, she realised with a spark of surprise. Fascinated her.

Would Zakari have done the same? The shadowy figure from her childhood held little appeal compared to the enigmatic presence of this man…this man, who was not and was never going to be her husband.

Aarif turned, his eyes clashing with hers, and Kalila jerked her gaze away, feeling exposed, as if he'd somehow witnessed her disturbing thought process.

'Kalila?' Bahir raised his eyebrow, drawing her back into the conversation.

'Please excuse me,' Kalila said quickly, forcing herself not to flush. 'My mind was else-where. Father?'

'Prince Aarif was just inquiring about bringing you to Calista. He wanted to leave tomorrow, and I was explaining to him about our customs.' Bahir smiled apologetically at Aarif. 'You see, Prince Aarif, there is a tradition here in Zaraq. The people love the royal family—it has always been so.' He paused and took a sip of wine. 'It is, perhaps, why we have enjoyed over a hundred years of peaceful rule.' It was, Kalila knew, a delicate reminder of the power and prestige Zaraq brought to this marriage alliance. 'The people of Makaris, our capital, like to hold a little festival when a member of the royal family is going to be married.' Bahir held up one smooth, well-manicured hand, anticipating Aarif's response, although he hadn't moved or spoken. He simply waited. 'I know this festival would normally occur after the wedding, but Kalila will be in Calista then, and it is important to the people that they see the happy couple...or at least the radiant bride.' There was no censure in Bahir's voice, but Aarif must have felt it for his mouth tightened once more.

'If my brother had been aware of such traditions, I am sure he would have made every effort to be here,' he said after a moment, and Bahir inclined his head in gracious acknowledgement.

'Of course, of course. As it is, he is not, and you are. And for the sake of our beloved people, as well as the peace of our happy country, the festival must go forward as planned. It is a small affair, a simple matter. Food, music, dancing. I thought, considering—' he paused delicately '—you could stop in Makaris on your way to the airport, and enjoy the festivities for an hour, two, no more. The people like a glimpse of the royal family, that is all.'

'On the way to the airport?' Aarif repeated, his voice scrupulously polite. 'It was my understanding we would depart from the palace's airstrip.'

Bahir waved a hand. 'Yes, yes, I can see how you would think that. But as I said, the people of Zaraq care very much for the royal family, and in truth Princess Kalila, being my only heir, is much loved. They will want to wish her well, say farewell, you know how it is.' He smiled, but no one could mistake the shrewd glint in his eyes.

Aarif dabbed his mouth with a napkin before smiling easily, although Kalila saw that his eyes were just as hard and shrewd as her father's. 'Yes, of course. We must satisfy the people, King Bahir. Let it be as you wish.'

Bahir smiled in satisfaction, and Kalila felt a sudden wave of numbing fatigue crash over her at the thought of several hours of mingling, chatting, waving, smiling. Indulging everyone's need for a fairy tale.

Yet it had to be done; it would be done. It was, she knew, all part of her duty as princess. As queen.

'I am sorry to rush you from your home, Princess,' Aarif said, turning to her. 'But as you know, the wedding is in two weeks, and there will be preparations to complete there.' He paused before adding almost as an afterthought, 'And of course King Zakari will be eager to see you, his bride.'

'Of course.' Kalila stared down at her untouched plate. At that moment she had trouble believing Zakari was eager for anything but another diamond in his crown.

The rest of the evening passed with more ease,

and Bahir made sure the wine and conversation flowed smoothly.

'I have heard that many of the Al'Farisi princes have been educated at Oxford,' he said as dessert, roasted plums seasoned with cardamom and nutmeg, was served. 'I went to Sandhurst myself, which is how I happened to meet my late wife, Queen Amelia, God rest her soul. Her brother was one of my best friends.' Bahir smiled in inquiry. 'Did you attend Oxford, Aarif?'

'I did, and then returned to Calista to oversee our diamond industry.'

'You are a man of business.'

'Indeed.'

And he looked like one, Kalila thought. All about hard facts and figures, details and prices. Even his eyes had the hardness of diamonds.

'Kalila went to Cambridge,' Bahir continued. 'As I'm sure you, or at least your brother, knows. She studied history, and enjoyed her years there, didn't you, my dear?'

'Yes, very much.' Kalila smiled stiffly, disliking the way her father trotted out her accomplishments as if she were a show pony. A brood mare.

'An education is important for any ruler, don't you think?' Bahir continued, and Aarif swivelled slightly to rest that harsh and unyielding gaze on Kalila.

She stilled under it, felt again that strange warmth bloom in her cheeks and her belly at his scrutiny. Strange, when his expression was so un-generous, his eyes so dark and obdurate. She should quell under that unyielding gaze, yet she didn't. She flourished. She wanted more, yet more of what? What more could a man like Aarif give?

'Yes,' he said flatly, and then looked away.

Finally the meal was over, and Bahir invited Aarif to take a cigar and port in his private study. It was a male tradition, one that took different guises all around the world, and all it took was for her father to raise his eyebrows at her for Kalila to know she'd been excused. It usually annoyed her, this arrogant dismissal of women from what was seen as the truly important matters, but tonight she was glad.

She wanted to be alone. She needed to think.

She waited until Bahir and Aarif were ensconced in the study before she slipped outside to the palace's private gardens, an oasis of verdant calm. She loved these gardens, the cool shade provided by a hundred different varieties of shrub and flower, the twisting paths that would suddenly lead to a fountain or sculpture or garden bench, some-thing pleasant and lovely.

She breathed in deeply the surprising scents of lavender and rose, imported from England by Bahir for the pleasure of his homesick wife.

The air was damp and fresh from the sprinkler system Bahir had installed, although Kalila could still feel the dry, creeping chill of the night-time desert air. She wished she'd thought to bring a wrap; her arms crept around her body instead.

She didn't want to marry Zakari. She acknowledged this starkly, peeled away the layers of self-deceit and foolish hope to reveal the plain and unpleasant truth underneath. She didn't want to travel to a foreign country, even one as close as Calista, to be a queen. She didn't want to live the life that had been carefully chosen for her too many years ago.

She didn't want to do her duty.

Funny, that she would realise this now. Now, when it was too late, far too late, when the wedding was imminent, the invitations already sent out even. Or were they? Funny, too, that she had no idea of the details of her own wedding, her own marriage, not even about the groom.

Kalila sighed. The path she'd been walking on opened onto a sheltered curve bound by hedgerows, set with a small fountain, its waters gleaming blackly in the darkness, the newly risen moon reflected on its still surface. She sank onto a bench by the fountain, curling her legs up to her chest and resting her chin on her knees, a position from childhood, a position of comfort.

From the ground she scooped up a handful of smooth pebbles and let them trickle through her fingers, each one making a tiny scuffling sound on the dirt below. She hadn't realised the truth of her situation until now, she knew, because she hadn't separated it from herself before.

Since she was a child of twelve—half of her life—she'd known she was going to marry King Zakari. She'd had a picture of him—from a newspaper—in her underwear drawer, although she made sure no one saw it. When she was alone, she'd taken it out and smoothed the paper, stared at the blurred image—it wasn't even a very good shot—and wondered about the man in the picture. The man who would be her husband, the father of her children, her life partner.

In those early years she'd embroidered delicate daydreams about him, his beauty and bravery, intelligence and humour. She'd built him up to be a king even before a crown rested on his head. Of course, that youthful naiveté hadn't lasted too long; by the time she went to Cambridge, she'd realised Zakari could not possibly be the man of her daydreams. No man could.

And even when she'd thought she was being realistic, nobly doing her duty, accepting the greater aims of her country, she'd still clung to those old daydreams. They'd hidden in the corner of her heart, dusty and determined, and only when Aarif had shown himself in the throne room had she realised their existence at all.

She still believed. She still *wanted*. She wanted that man…impossible, wonderful, somehow real.

Because that man loved her…whoever he was.

For a strange, surprised moment, Aarif's implacable features flashed through her mind, and she shook her head as if to deny what a secret part of her brain was telling her. The only reason she thought of Aarif at all, she told herself, was because Zakari wasn't here.

Yet she couldn't quite rid herself of the lingering sense of his presence, that faint flicker of his smile. *You wore a white dress, with a bow in your hair.*

Such a simple statement, and yet there had been a strange intimacy in that memory, in its revelation.

'Excuse me.'

The voice, sharp and sudden, caused Kalila to stiffen in surprise. Aarif stood by the fountain, no more than a shadowy form in the darkness. They stared at each other, the only sound the rustling of leaves and, in the distance, the gentle churring of a nightjar.

'I didn't realise,' Aarif said after a moment, his voice stiff and formal, 'that anyone was here.'

Kalila swallowed. 'I thought you'd still be with my father.'

'We finished, and he wished to go to bed.'

More time must have passed than she'd realised, lost in her own unhappy reflections.

'I'll go,' Aarif said, and began to turn.

'Please. Don't.' The words came out in a rush, surprising her. Kalila didn't know what she wanted from this man, so hard and strange and ungiving. Yet she knew she didn't want him to go; she didn't want to be alone any more. She wanted, she realised, to be with him. To know more about him, even if there was no point. No purpose.

Aarif hesitated, still half-turned, and then as Kalila held her breath he slowly swivelled back to her. In the darkness she couldn't see his expression. 'Is there something I can help you with, Princess?'

Kalila patted the empty seat next to her. 'Please sit.'

Another long moment passed, and in the darkness Kalila thought she could see Aarif gazing thoughtfully at that empty space before he moved slowly—reluctantly—and sat down next to her, yet still far enough apart so his body did not touch hers at all.

The constraint of his behaviour, Kalila realised, was revealing in itself. Was he aware of the tension Kalila felt, that heady sense of something unfurling within her, something she'd never felt before?

Did he feel it too?

He couldn't, Kalila decided, or if he did, he was not showing it. He sat rigidly, his hands resting on his thighs, unmoving, and it amazed her how still and controlled he was, giving nothing away by either sound or movement.

'This is a beautiful garden,' Aarif said after a moment, and Kalila was glad he'd spoken.

'I have always loved it,' she agreed quietly. 'My father designed it for my mother—a taste of her homeland.'

'Like the Gardens of Babylon, built by Nebuchadnezzar for Amytis.'

'Yes.' Kalila smiled, pleased he'd recognised the connection. 'My father used to call my mother Amytis, as an endearment.' She heard the wistful note in her voice and bit her lip.

'I'm sorry for her death,' Aarif said, his voice still formal and somehow remote. 'The loss of a parent is a hard thing to bear.'

'Yes.'

'When did she die?'

'When I was seventeen. Cancer.' Kalila swallowed. It had been so unexpected, so swift. There had only been a few, precious, painful weeks between diagnosis and death, and then the raging emptiness afterwards. Going to Cambridge had been a relief, a new beginning, and yet Kalila knew the ache of her mother's loss would never fully heal. It was something you carried with you, always.

'I'm sorry,' Aarif said quietly, and Kalila knew he meant it. Above them the nightjar began its steady churring once more.

'I know you lost your father and stepmother a few years ago,' she said hesitantly. 'I…I heard of it. I'm sorry.' She'd written to Zakari, she remembered, expressing her condolences, and she'd received a formal letter back. Now she wondered if he'd even written it.

'Thank you. It was…difficult.' Aarif said nothing more, and Kalila did not feel she could brave the intimacy of asking. He shifted slightly, and she wondered if he was uncomfortable. There was a strange, quiet intimacy provided by the cloak of darkness, the sounds of the night gentle and hypnotic around them. She wished she could see his face, but the moon had gone beyond a cloud and she could see no more than the shadowy outline of his shoulder, his jaw, his cheek.

'Tell me about Calista,' she finally said. 'You know, I've never been there.'

Aarif was silent for so long Kalila wondered if he'd heard her. 'It's beautiful,' he finally said. 'Much like here.' He paused, and Kalila waited. 'Of course, not everyone sees the beauty of the desert. It is a harsh loveliness. Was it difficult for your mother to live here?'

'Sometimes,' Kalila acknowledged. 'Although she took trips back to England—I spent my first holidays in Bournemouth.'

The moon glided out from behind a cloud, and in the pale light Kalila saw his teeth gleam, and she realised he was smiling. Faintly. The gesture surprised her; he hadn't smiled properly since she'd met him. She wished she could see more of it. She wondered if the smile lit his eyes, softened the hard planes of his face, and realised she wanted to know. 'And she had the garden, of course,' she finished after a moment, her voice sounding stilted. 'She loved it here.'

'And you?' Aarif asked. 'Will you miss your homeland?'

Kalila swallowed. 'Yes…I think so.' He said nothing, but she felt his silent censure like a physical thing, tautening the small space between them. And, of course, why shouldn't he be surprised? Disappointed even? Here she was, admitting that she didn't know if she'd miss her own country! She opened her mouth, wanting to explain the jumble of confused emotions and disappointed dreams to him, but nothing came out. What could she say, and what would this man want to hear?

Yet somehow, strangely, she felt as if he might understand. Or was that simply the wishful thinking of a woman with too many disappointed dreams?

'I'll miss Zaraq, of course,' she said, after a moment, wanting, needing to explain. 'And my father. And friends…' She trailed off, unable to put words to the nameless longing for something else, something deeper and more instrinsically a part of herself, something that had no name. Something, she realised despondently, she wasn't even sure she'd ever had.

'It is a strange time,' Aarif said after a moment. His voice was still neutral, yet in the shadowy darkness Kalila saw him lift his hand and drop it again—almost as if he'd been going to touch her. Her heart beat harder at the thought. 'Once you are in Calista, you will feel more settled. The people will welcome you.' He paused before adding, his voice still flat, 'I'm sure they will love you.'

The people. Not Zakari. And what of him? What of Aarif? The question was ludicrous, so ridiculous and inappropriate that under the cover of darkness Kalila's cheeks warmed. 'Thank you,' she whispered. 'I suppose I sound like I am full of self-pity, but I hope—I know—' she swallowed painfully '—that it will be better with time.'

'Time heals most things,' Aarif agreed, yet Kalila felt he was saying something else, something far from a platitude. Most things…but not all.

Aarif stirred on the bench and Kalila knew he wanted to leave. The night had grown quiet, their conversation too close. Yet the thought of his departure alarmed her, and she held out one hand, the moonlight bathing her skin in lambent silver. 'Tell me about your brother.'

The words fell in the silence like the pebbles from her hand, disturbing the tranquil stillness. Kalila wished she hadn't spoken. Why had she asked about Zakari? She didn't want to know about him. She didn't even want to *think* about him.

But you need to know. He is going to be your husband.

'What kind of man is he?' she asked, her voice trailing to a whisper. It shamed her that she had to ask. She felt as if she'd exposed something to Aarif without even realising it, as much as if she'd shown him that faded photograph in her lingerie drawer.

'He is a good man,' Aarif said after a long moment when he'd remained still and silent, his head half turned away from her. 'A better man than I am. And a good king.' Kalila started at his admission. *A better man than I am. Why? What kind of man are you?* She wanted to ask, but she was silent, and Aarif finished, 'He will do his duty.'

His duty. Highest praise, no doubt, from a man like Aarif, but to Kalila it had the ring of condemnation. She wanted so much more than duty. Summoning her spirit, she tried for a laugh. 'Can't you tell me more than that?' she asked, keeping her voice light.

Aarif turned to look at her, his eyes and face carefully expressionless. 'I fear I cannot tell you the kinds of things a bride would like to know about her groom. And in truth, you will know soon enough.'

'I thought he would have come. To see me.' Kalila bit her lip, wishing the words back. Then she shrugged, a sudden spark of defiance firing through her. 'He should have.'

Aarif stiffened, or at least Kalila felt as if he had. Perhaps he hadn't moved at all. Yet she knew she'd gone too far; she'd almost insulted King Zakari. Her husband. She closed her eyes, opening them once more when Aarif spoke.

'It was my fault that you were expecting King Zakari,' he told her flatly. 'I should have explained the arrangements before my arrival.'

Kalila glanced at him, curiosity flaring within her. Aarif held himself rigidly now, and although he was still unmoving she felt his tension emanating from him in forceful waves. He was not the kind of man to make such a mistake, she reflected, so what had happened? Why was he taking the blame?

'It is no matter,' she said after a moment. She could hardly explain how much it had mattered, or why. 'King Zakari will be waiting for me in Calista. The wedding has already been delayed several times—what is a few more days?'

'It seems,' Aarif replied, his voice carefully neutral, 'that it matters to you.'

Kalila looked away. That afternoon, it had mattered. She had been disappointed, hurt, like the child at a birthday party Aarif had thought her, waiting for a present only to find it empty inside. Yet now she felt worse; she was numb, indifferent. She'd finally realised there had never been a present, or even a façade of a present. There had only been an empty box.

And there was nothing she could do about it.

'Princess Kalila, I should go.' Aarif rose from the bench. 'It is not seemly for us to be like this.'

'Why not? We shall be as brother and sister in a matter of weeks,' Kalila replied, raising her eyebrows in challenge.

Aarif paused. 'True, but you know as well as I do that in countries such as ours men and women who are unattached do not spend time alone together, unchaperoned.'

'Are you unattached?' The question slipped out without much thought, yet Kalila realised she wanted to know. He wasn't married, but was there a woman? A girlfriend, a mistress, a lover?

She shouldn't ask; she didn't need to know. Yet she wanted to. Something about that still, considering gaze, the carefully neutral tone, made her want to know the man that must be hidden underneath.

'Yes.' Aarif made to turn. 'And now I must bid you goodnight. I trust you can find your way safely back to the palace?'

'Yes—' Half-turned as he was, the moonlight bathing his cheek in silver, illuminating that livid line from brow to jaw, Kalila found another question slipping out. 'How did you get that scar?'

Aarif jerked in surprise, and then he turned slowly to face her. From the surprised—almost trapped—look on his face Kalila realised it was not a question she should have asked. It was not one Aarif wanted to answer. Still, she waited, her breath caught in her throat, her mind a flurry of questions.

'A foolish accident,' Aarif finally said, stiffly, as if he were not used to explaining. Perhaps he wasn't.

'It must have been.' She regarded him solemnly, longing to lighten the moment, to make him smile again—somehow. 'You look as if someone came at you with a scimitar,' she added, letting a teasing note enter her voice. 'Did you win?' She held her breath, waiting for his reaction.

After an endless moment Aarif's mouth curved in a tiny, reluctant smile. That hint of humour caused Kalila's heart to lurch, her insides to roil in a confused jumble, for suddenly he did not seem like the man he'd been before. Suddenly he seemed like someone else entirely. Someone she wanted to know, the man underneath she'd wondered about coming to the fore.

'Would you believe me,' he asked, 'if I told you I took on three camel rustlers by myself?'

His gaze was steady on hers, his mouth still curved. Kalila smiled and nodded. 'Yes, I would.'

And suddenly the moment of levity took on a deeper, disquieting meaning; suddenly something was stretching between them, winding around them, drawing them closer though neither of them moved.

Aarif's eyes held hers and she didn't look away. She reached one hand out in farewell, and to her surprise Aarif clasped it, his fingers, dry and cool, wrapping around hers, sending a jolt of startling awareness along her arm and through her whole body.

Her fingers tightened on his, and as the moment stretched on—too long—neither one of them let go. Neither of them, Kalila felt, wanted to. She should have pulled her hand away. Aarif should have loosened his grip.

Yet neither of them did, and the moment stretched on suspended and endless, as they remained, linked by their clasped fingers, holding each other's gaze with a silent, suppressed longing. Kalila felt a clamour of different emotions rise within her: the need to be understood, cherished. Loved. The idea, strange and impossible, that this man could be the one who would.

Then, as if rousing himself from a dream, Aarif shook his head, the light in his eyes replaced by an even more disquieting bleakness, his mouth returning to its familiar, compressed line. He dropped her hand so suddenly Kalila's arm swung down helplessly in the darkness, landing in her lap with a thud. She curled her fingers, now burning with the memory of his touch, against her thigh as Aarif turned away.

'Goodnight, Princess,' he said, and disappeared silently into the darkness of the garden.

CHAPTER THREE

BY THE time Kalila awoke the next morning the city was alive with excitement and activity. She could sense it from the window of her dressing room, which faced east towards Makaris. She smelled it on the wind carried from the city, the scents of frying meat and spices, felt it in the air as if it were a tangible thing.

Kalila felt an answering excitement in herself, although her mind skittered away from its source. She was not looking forward to her marriage, yet she found herself eagerly anticipating the journey to Calista. With Aarif.

Stop. She shouldn't think like this, want like this. Yet the desires she felt were formless, nameless, and Kalila knew it was better for them to stay that way. Safer. In a fortnight, she would marry Zakari. There was no escaping that fate. Yet if she could afford herself a few brief, harmless moments of pleasure before then—

Stop.

'Kalila! It is time you dressed!' Juhanah bustled in, clapping her hands as she beamed in excitement. She would be accompanying her to Calista, and would stay for as long as it took for Kalila to settle.

And how long would that be? Kalila wondered, feeling the familiar despair settle over her once more. Days, months, years? Ever?

'Kalila, my princess.' Juhanah knelt by her side as Kalila sat on the window seat, one shoulder propped against the stone frame. 'It is time. Prince Aarif wishes your bags to be loaded, everything is prepared.'

'Already?' She turned away from the window. Her clothes and personal items had already been packed; many of them she'd left in boxes, shipped from England. She did not have too much to bring, clothes, a few books and photographs, nothing more. They felt like scraps being brought to a feast, a humble and pathetic offering.

'Juhanah, I don't want to go.' The words tumbled from her and her lips trembled. She pressed them together tightly, willed herself not to cry. Tears, now, would do no good. Still, she had to speak. She needed to give voices to the nameless terrors clamouring within her. 'I don't want to marry him,' she whispered.

Juhanah was silent for a moment. Kalila couldn't look at her; she felt too ashamed. 'Oh, *ya daanaya,*' Juhanah finally said, and rose to put her arms around Kalila. Kalila rested her head against Juhanah's pillowy bosom, let herself be comforted like a child. 'Of course you are afraid now. If King Zakari had come, perhaps it would be different. It is a hard thing, to travel to a strange country and wed a strange man.'

'But I don't think it *would* be different,' Kalila whispered. 'I realised that last night. I don't want to do it, Juhanah. I don't care what he's like. He doesn't love me.'

'In time—'

'In time comes affection, understanding, kindness,' Kalila cut her off. '*Maybe.* I've been telling myself that for years. But why should I settle for such things? My father was able to have a love match. Aarif's father and stepmother—Anya and Ashraf—had a love match. Why not me?'

Juhanah released her, her mouth pursed thoughtfully. '*Aarif's* father?' she repeated, and Kalila flushed.

'Zakari's father as well. Why must I settle?'

'You are doing a great thing for your country,' Juhanah told her, and there was a warning note in her nurse's voice that reminded Kalila of when she'd been caught stealing honey cakes from the kitchen. 'You must act like the princess you are, Kalila, and do your duty.'

'Yes. I know.' She'd accepted that many years

ago, had told herself it many times. Yet all those resolutions crumbled to dust in face of the harsh, present reality. 'I know,' she repeated, and if Juhanah heard the damning waver of doubt in Kalila's voice, she did not comment on it.

'Now, come. You must dress.'

'I'm not wearing another costume,' Kalila warned. 'I won't truss myself up like a harem girl so the people of Makaris can be satisfied.'

'Of course not,' Juhanah soothed. 'Besides, it wouldn't be sensible for travel.'

Kalila gave a little laugh, and Juhanah smiled encouragingly. She was wound so tightly, so desperately, she realised, and that little laugh reminded her of who she was. Who she used to be. She was a girl who laughed, who loved life, who embraced each opportunity with pleasure, abandon.

She was not this skittish, frightened, desperate creature. She would not let herself be.

In the end she chose a pair of loose cotton trousers and a matching tunic in palest green, embroidered with silver thread. She plaited her hair once more, and wore silver hoops on her ears, a silver locket that had been her mother's around her neck.

Juhanah went to supervise the packing, and Kalila was left alone in her childhood bedroom. In a few moments she would say goodbye to the palace, the staff, and then her father. Bahir would fly to Calista for the wedding, but it wouldn't be the same. When she walked out of the palace, she would be leaving this life for ever.

The thought saddened her. She'd grown up here, explored the echoing, shadowy corridors, curled up in a sunny window seat, sneaked into her father's library or the palace kitchen. The first time she'd been away from home for any length of time had been when she'd gone to Cambridge.

And what a different life she'd had there! A shared flat with a few other girls, nights out at the pub or takeaway pizza and a bottle of wine, everything casual and messy and fun.

She felt as if she were two people, the princess and the person. The queen-in-waiting and the modern girl who just wanted to be loved.

Yet you couldn't be two people and still be happy. Still be yourself. So how would she survive in the coming months and years, when she took on the mantle that was so foreign to her, queen, wife? How could she be happy?

Again Aarif's image flittered through her mind, tempting, treacherous. She'd been happy in his presence. She shook her head as if to deny herself that forbidden truth, and left her bedroom. From the window in the upstairs corridor she saw a motorcade assembled in the palace courtyard. There was a van for her cases, a car for Aarif, another for her father, a car for her and Juhanah, and another for the palace staff accompanying them to the airport.

It was a parade, and she was the centrepiece. Kalila closed her eyes. Her fingers curled around the sun-warmed stone of the window sill, and she held onto it like an anchor.

'I can't do it,' she whispered aloud, though there was no one to hear. Her own heart heard, and answered. *I won't.*

The sun beat down on Aarif as he stood in the palace courtyard, waiting for Kalila to arrive. A light wind blowing from the desert eased his discomfort, and he was grateful for the refreshment. He'd been up since dawn, seeing to arrangements; he wanted nothing left to chance or circumstance, no more mistakes to be made.

The first one had been bad enough.

Aarif's mouth twisted in a grimace as he recalled his private interview with King Bahir last night, after dinner. The king was too shrewd and politic to be overt about his displeasure, but he'd made his disappointment over Zakari's absence known.

Aarif had done his best to be apologetic without weakening his own position, or that of his brother. He half-wondered if Bahir was making a bigger to-do about Zakari's absence than perhaps was warranted; it could be, in future, a necessary bargaining chip.

And what of Kalila? His mind drifted back to the evening in the garden, the scent of roses mixed with a heady scent that he felt—feared—was the princess herself. He'd watched her out of the corner of his eye as he'd sat on the bench, less than a foot away from her. He'd seen how the moonlight had gleamed on her heavy, dark hair; he'd found his eyes drawn to the bare, graceful curve of her neck.

He'd felt her fingers in his, and he had not wanted to stop touching her. It had been a balm, that gentle touch, as if she'd understood him. As if she'd wanted to.

Yet even more than her appearance or touch had been her words, her smile. *You look as if someone came at you with a scimitar.* No one talked about his scar, no one asked him to remember. No one made him smile.

Except, somehow, inexplicably, she had. She'd slipped under his defences without even knowing she'd done so, and it made him both uneasy and strangely glad.

Stop. His mind clamped down on these wandering thoughts with the precision and power of a steel trap. He had no business thinking of Kalila's neck or hair, wondering what she smelled like, remembering the feel of her fingers. He had no business thinking of her at all.

She was to be his brother's wife. He was here as a proxy, a servant, and he would do his job, fulfil his task.

He wouldn't fail.

There was a flurry of movement at the palace doors, and Aarif saw Kalila come out into the courtyard. Her father was behind her, dressed simply as Aarif was, in a white cotton shirt and tan chinos.

It was too hot, Aarif acknowledged, for formal dress. And his sense of the festival in Makaris was that it was a fun, light-hearted affair, a celebration rather than a ceremony.

Kalila approached him, looking fresh and cool, her eyes bright and clear, her smile firmly in place. As she came closer he saw shadows under her eyes, and her smile started to look a little fixed. She was bound to be a bit nervous, he supposed, a bit uncertain.

'Good morning, Princess.'

'Prince Aarif.' She gave a small, graceful nod. 'Thank you for helping with these arrangements. You do me a great service.'

Aarif sketched a short bow back. 'It is my honour and pleasure.'

The formalities dealt with, she lowered her voice. 'Thank you for your conversation in the garden last night. It helped me immeasurably.'

Aarif felt himself grow cold, his formal smile

turning rigid. He felt as if her simple thanks had cast a sordid, revealing light on that innocent conversation—for it hadn't been innocent, had it? His thoughts hadn't, his touch hadn't.

He nodded brusquely, saw the flicker of disappointed hurt in her eyes before she nodded back, accepting. He turned to gaze at the line of shiny black cars. 'The day grows old and the sun high. We should not delay, for the people of Makaris are eager, I am sure.'

Kalila folded her arms protectively across her middle before becoming aware of the defensive position and dropping them. 'Tell me, will King Zakari be in Calista when I arrive?' Aarif hesitated, and she met his gaze knowingly. 'Will he be waiting at the airport with a bouquet of roses, do you think?' He heard the thread of mockery in her voice and felt equal stabs of annoyance and alarm. Did the girl actually expect a love match? Was she that naive, or simply hopeful?

Didn't she deserve one?

He made his voice non-committal. 'I am sure King Zakari will be pleased to renew your acquaintance.'

'If you ring him to tell him,' Kalila said, and now he heard laughter in her voice, brittle and sharp, 'tell him I don't actually like roses. Irises are my favourite.'

Aarif did not answer, and she moved away, her body held with stiff dignity. He suppressed another prickle of irritation. The last thing he needed was a royal princess's hurt feelings to deal with. Surely she'd known this was an alliance of countries, not some great romance! Yet apparently she'd been hoping for something of the sort, or so it had seemed last night, when he'd heard the aching disappointment in her voice…

Aarif turned his mind resolutely away from the memory of last night, the quiet, forbidden intimacy of the garden. He turned to one of the palace staff who waited patiently for orders.

'Have the cases been loaded?' he demanded, hearing his tone and knowing it was unnecessarily surly and abrupt.

The aide lowered his eyes. 'Yes, Prince Aarif.'

'Good.' Aarif glanced at the sky, the endless blue smudged by a faint streak of grimy grey on the horizon. 'It looks like a wind is kicking up. We should leave without delay.'

It was another half-hour before they actually began to drive the five kilometers to Makaris, as servants and staff hurried to and fro, remembering this, forgetting that, while Aarif waited and watched, curbing his irritation with effort.

He wanted this whole spectacle to be finished. He wanted to be back in Calista, in his offices, away from the distractions, the temptations—

Again his mind clamped down, and he shook his head. No, he wouldn't think of it. Of her.

As the motorcade moved into Makaris people lined the road, and the cars slowed to a crawl. Ahead of him Aarif saw Kalila's car window open, and a slender, golden arm emerge to accept ragged bouquets of flowers, scraps of paper printed with blessings and prayers, and other well wishes. The crowd smiled, cheered, and called their blessings, children and dogs trailing the cars as they went under the main arch of the city into the Old Town, with its crumbling buildings of red clay, before emerging into a large square lined with food stalls and filled to near overflowing with a joyous throng.

The cars drew to a halt, and King Bahir emerged from the front car, smiling and waving while aides stayed close to his side. Aarif looked around the ragged crowd with a deepening unease.

It was crowded, dirty, impossible to keep track of Kalila. Anyone could accost her, anything could happen. Aarif knew how quickly it could all go desperately, dreadfully wrong. And he, Aarif, would be responsible. Again.

He threw open the door of his car, snapping to an aide behind him. 'Stay close to the princess. Don't let her out of your sight.'

The man nodded, scurrying off, and Aarif stood in the centre of the square, shielding his eyes from the glare of the sun as people pressed close, desperate for a glimpse of the royals, a blessing from the princess.

A space had been cleared for dancing, and Aarif watched as some local women put on a little show, a band of men in colorful robes and turbans playing instruments, the bandir drum, the maqrunah, the garagab. Together the instruments made a reedy, dissonant, not unpleasing sound, yet with the crowds and the heavy, spicy smell of fried food from the stalls, Aarif found himself annoyed, tensing, on alert.

There was too much risk. Too much danger. It kicked his heart-rate up a notch, made his palms slick with sweat. He despised himself for it; he despised his fear.

He despised the uncertainty, the unknown.

Anything could happen here.

He glanced around, his eyes sifting through the crowds, and saw Kalila standing at the front of the cleared space, watching the little dance as if it completely captured her attention. Her hair fell down her back in a dark, gleaming plait, and the breeze moulded her loose clothing to her body, so Aarif could see the gentle swell of her breast and hip. He swallowed, dragging his gaze away.

Next to him a ragged little boy tugged on his leg, and Aarif glanced down at his smiling face and reached for a coin, glad for the distraction.

The presentation ended, and once again Aarif found his gaze pulled relentlessly back to the princess. She clapped and smiled, speaking to each woman in turn, her arm around them as if they were equals. Friends.

Aarif felt a reluctant tug of admiration for her poise. He knew she was under strain, nervous and tense, and yet she acted with an innate grace. She acted like the princess she was, the queen she would be. His brother's wife.

He turned away, scouring the crowds on the other side for any sign of danger, darkness—

'The king wishes you to join him and the princess,' an aide murmured in his ear, bowing low, and Aarif was left with little choice than to make his way through the crowds to King Bahir's—and Kalila's—side.

She glanced at him sideways as he approached, smiling slightly, and Aarif gave a tiny bow back. Her smile deepened, but her eyes, those deep golden pools of reflected emotion and light, were sad, and Aarif felt something inside him tug, something start to unravel. He wanted to make her smile. He pushed the feeling away, and when Kalila looked back at the dancers so did Aarif.

The dance was followed by another, and then a performance by children. Aarif watched, feeling himself grow weary even as Kalila continued to smile and applaud, speaking individually to each man, woman, and child. Finally the performances ended, and Aarif realised a meal of sorts was to be served.

Perhaps after they'd eaten they would be free to continue to the airport, and finally home. Safety.

Makeshift tables and benches, no more than rough planks, had been set up by the food stalls, and Kalila and her father sat down with a few other important dignitaries from the palace. A few well-placed individuals from the city crowd had been chosen as well, Aarif saw with a cynical smile, a pretty child, a smiling old woman, a fat merchant.

The food was served, dish after dish of beef kebabs and chicken with raisins and rice, stewed prunes and eggplant salad. Aarif ate a bit of everything so as not to offend, although his nerves were wound too tightly to enjoy what was a surprisingly delicious meal.

The plates were cleared and the music and dancing began once again in the square, with no sign of the festivities abating. Aarif suppressed a sigh of impatience, nerves tautening like wire. He was hot and sticky, tense and irritable, and they'd already been there too long. It was time to take charge.

He wove his way over to Bahir, who was smiling at some of the more energetic dancing that was now going on, men in a circle with their arms crossed, stamping their feet. Instinctively Aarif looked around for Kalila, but her slight figure was nowhere to be seen.

He scanned the crowded market place, the crush

of bodies, searching for her distinctive figure, that gleaming plait of hair, knowing instinctively if she was there, certain he could find her.

She wasn't there. He knew it, felt it like a shock to his system, rippling unpleasantly through him. Somehow, somewhere, she had gone. A sharp pain stabbed him in the gut, memory and anger and fear. Aarif's mouth tightened, his eyes narrowed against the dazzling glare of the sun.

He saw Bahir glance at him in question, but Aarif did not want to see the older man now. He wanted to see Kalila. He wanted to know she was safe. He needed to.

He pushed away from Bahir, through the crowds, scanning the strange, smiling faces for a glimpse of the untarnished loveliness he'd seen in the garden last night.

Where was she?

He caught sight of the aide he'd assigned as her babysitter, and grabbed the man's elbow. 'Where is the princess?' he demanded roughly.

The aide flinched under Aarif's rough grasp. 'She went into the church for some cool air. I thought there was no harm—'

Aarif swore under his breath and let the man go. His gaze searched the square before he found what he was looking for—an ancient church in the Byzantine style, made of a startling white stone with a blue cross on top of its dome. He moved towards it with grim purpose.

The door was partly ajar, and Aarif slipped inside quietly. The church was refreshingly cool and dark, and empty save for a few benches and some icons adorning the walls. Kalila sat on one of the benches, her back to Aarif. Something about her position—the rigid set of her shoulders and yet the despairing bowing of her head—made Aarif pause.

He took a breath, waited for the rush of fury to recede, acknowledging to himself it had been unwarranted. Too much. And yet for a moment he'd thought—he remembered—

He cleared his throat, and Kalila turned her head so her face was in profile, her dark lashes sweeping her cheek. 'Have you come to take me away?' she asked, her voice soft, as if it were being absorbed by the stone.

Aarif took a step towards her. 'I wondered where you were.'

'I wished for some air.' She paused, and Aarif waited. 'I've always liked this place. My parents were married here, you know. It was founded when the Byzantines went down to Africa—well over a thousand years ago now.' She gave a little sigh as she looked around the bare walls. 'It survived the invasion of the Berbers, the Ottomans, the Turks. A noble task, don't you think, to keep one's identity amidst so much change?'

Aarif took a step closer to her. 'Indeed, as your country has done,' he said, choosing to guide the conversation to more impersonal waters. 'I know the history of Zaraq well, Princess, as it is a neighbour of my own homeland, Calista. When nearly every other kingdom was invaded and taken over the centuries, yours alone survived.'

'Yes, because we didn't have anything anyone wanted.' She gave a little laugh that sounded cynical and somehow wrong. 'Ringed by mountains, little more than desert, and inhabited by a fierce people willing to fight to the death for their pathetic patch of land. It's no wonder we survived, at least until the French came and realised there was nickel and copper to be had under our barren earth.'

'Your independence is no small thing,' Aarif said. He saw Kalila's hands bunch into fists in her lap.

'No, it isn't,' she agreed in a voice that surprised him; it was steely and sure. 'I'm glad you realise that.'

Aarif hesitated. He felt the ripple of tension and something deeper, something dark and determined from Kalila, and he wondered at its source.

In an hour, he reminded himself, they would be on a plane. In three hours, they could be at the Calistan palace, and Kalila would be kept in the women's quarters, safe with her old nurse, away from him. The thought should have comforted him; he'd meant it to. Instead he felt the betraying, wrenching pain of loss.

'We have enjoyed the festivities, Princess,' he said, 'but you were right, we must go. The hour grows late and a storm looks to approach, a sirocco, and living in the desert you know how dangerous they can be.'

'A storm?' Interest lifted Kalila's voice momentarily. 'Will the plane be delayed, do you think?'

'Not if we leave promptly.'

She hesitated, and Aarif resisted the urge to take her into his arms. He wanted to scold her, tell her to stop feeling sorry for herself, and yet he also wanted to comfort her, to breathe in the scent of her hair—

Irritated by his own impulse, he sharpened his tone. 'I regret to disturb your tranquillity, Princess, but there is a duty to fulfil.' There always was, no matter how crippling the weight, how difficult the task.

'I'm coming,' she said at last, and there was a new resolute determination to her tone that relieved Aarif. She rose gracefully, glanced at him, her eyes fastening on his, and once again Aarif was transfixed by that clear gaze, yet this time he couldn't read the expression in it.

'I'm sorry, Prince Aarif,' she said in a quiet, steady voice, 'for any trouble I've caused you.'

She laid a hand on his arm, her fingers slender and cool, yet burning Aarif's skin. Branding it, and he resisted the desire to cover her hand with his own, to feel her fingers twine with his once more. A simple, seductive touch.

He raised his eyebrows in surprise before managing a cool smile. 'There has been no trouble, Princess.' Carefully, deliberately, he moved his arm away from her touch.

Her hand dropped to her side, and she smiled back as if she didn't believe him, going so far as to give her head a little shake, before she moved out of the cool church into the dusty heat of the crowded square.

The festivities were blessedly winding down by the time they found their way back to the royal party. Aarif was glad to see Kalila's—and his— absence had not been noted, although Bahir gave them both a quick, sharp glance before indulging the crowd in a formal farewell of his daughter. He kissed both her cheeks and bestowed his blessing; while they went on to the national airport, he would return to the palace.

Kalila accepted his farewell with dignity, her head bowed, and then turned to enter her car. Everyone followed suit, the doors closed, and with a sigh of relief Aarif saw they were at last on their way. Surely nothing could go wrong now.

The cars moved slowly through the crowded

streets of the Old Town, still chased by a merry crowd of well wishers, then back onto the main boulevard, a straight, flat road lined with dusty palm trees that led to the airport.

The airport was only ten kilometres away, but Aarif noted the darkening smudge on the horizon with some dismay. How long would it take to load all of the cases, make any arrangements? He knew well enough how these things could drag on.

As if to prove his point, the cars slowly drew to a halt. Aarif rolled down his window and peered ahead, but through the dust kicked up by the line of cars he could see nothing.

A minute passed and nothing moved. With another muttered oath, Aarif threw open his door and strode down the barren road to the princess's car.

He rapped twice on the window and after a moment Kalila's nurse, a plump woman with bright eyes and rounded cheeks, rolled down the window.

'Prince Aarif!'

'Is the princess well?' Aarif asked. 'Do you know why we are stopped?'

'She felt ill,' the nurse gabbled. 'And asked to be given a moment…of privacy…'

A sudden shadow of foreboding fell over Aarif, far more ominous than the storm gathering on the horizon. He thought of his conversation with Kalila only moments ago in the church, her talk of independence, her apology for troubling him, and the shadow of foreboding intensified into a throbbing darkness.

'Where is she?' he asked, and heard the harsh grating of his own voice. The nurse looked both alarmed and offended, and drew back. Aarif gritted his teeth and tried for patience. 'This is not a safe place, madam. I do not trust her security in such an inhospitable location.' He glanced up; the smudge on the horizon was growing darker, wider. Makaris was at least five kilometres behind them, and rocky desert stretched in every direction, the flat landscape marked only by large, tumbled boulders, as if thrown by a giant, unseen hand.

The nurse hesitated, and Aarif felt his frustration growing. He wanted to shake the silly woman, to demand answers—

'She's over there.' The woman pointed a shaking finger to a cluster of rocks about twenty metres away. A perfect hiding place.

Aarif strode towards them, his body taut with purpose and fury. He didn't know why he felt so angry, so afraid. Perhaps Kalila did indeed need a moment of privacy. Perhaps she was ill. Perhaps this was all in his mind, paranoid, pathetic. Remembering.

Yet he couldn't ignore his instinct; it was too strong, too insistent, a relentless drumming in his head, his heart.

Something had gone wrong. Something always went wrong.

Still, as he approached the rocks he hesitated. If Kalila was indeed in an indelicate position, it would not do to disturb her. Yet if she was in danger, or worse...

What was worse? What could be worse than danger?

Yet even as Aarif turned the corner of the rocky outcropping, he knew. He knew just what nameless fear had clutched at him since Kalila had apologised in the church, or perhaps even before then, when he'd heard her unhappy sigh in the garden.

For on the other side of the rocks, there was nothing, no princess. But on the horizon, riding towards the storm, was a lone figure on a horse.

Kalila, Aarif realised grimly, was running away.

CHAPTER FOUR

KALILA knew where she was going. It was that thought that sustained her as the wind whipped the headscarf around her face and the gritty sand stung her eyes. She pictured the scene behind her, how quickly it would erupt into chaos, and felt a deep shaft of guilt pierce her.

How long would it take Aarif to realise she had gone? And what would he do? Even with her brief acquaintance of the man, Kalila knew instinctively what the desert prince would do. He would go after her.

The thought sent a shiver of apprehension straight through her, and she clenched her hands on the reins. Arranging her disappearance had not been easy; the plan had crystallised only that morning when she'd looked down at the courtyard, seen the dismantling of her life, and realised she couldn't do it. She couldn't ride like a sacrifice to Calista, to marry a man she didn't love, didn't even know. Not yet, anyway.

Yet even as she rode towards a grim horizon, an uncertain future, she knew this freedom couldn't last for ever. She couldn't live in the desert like a nomad; Aarif would find her, and if he didn't someone else would.

Yet still she ran. That was what fear did to you, she supposed. It made you miserable, sick, dizzy. Desperate. Willing to do anything, try anything, no matter how risky or foolish, how thoughtless or selfish.

So she kept riding, heading for the one place she knew she'd be safe…at least for a little while.

Two kilometres behind her Aarif grimly wound a turban around his head to protect himself from the dust. Already the wind was kicking grit into his eyes, stinging his cheeks. What was she thinking, he wondered furiously, to ride out in weather like this? He'd warned her of the storm, and surely, as a child of a desert, she knew the dangers.

So was she stupid, he wondered with savage humour, or just desperate?

It didn't matter. She had to be found. He'd already sent an aide back to fetch a horse and provisions from the city.

The aide had been appalled. 'But King Bahir must be notified! He will send out a search party—'

Aarif gestured to the darkening sky. 'There is no time for a search party. The princess must be found, and as soon as possible. I will go…alone.' He watched the aide's eyes widen at this suggestion of impropriety. 'Circumstances are dire,' he informed the man flatly. 'If the princess is not found, it will be all of your necks on the line.' And his. He thought of Zakari, of Bahir, of the countries and families depending on him bringing Kalila back to Calista, and another fresh wave of fury surged through him.

'Prince Aarif!' A man jogged up to his elbow. 'There is a horse, and some water and bread and meat. We could not get anything else in such a hurry—'

'Good.' Aarif shrugged into the long, cotton *thobe* he wore to protect his clothes from the onslaught of the sun and sand. He'd exchanged his shoes for sturdy boots, and now he swung up onto the back of the horse, a capable if elderly mount.

'Drive to the airport,' he instructed the aide, 'and shelter there until the storm wears out. Do not contact the king.' His mouth curved in a grim smile. 'We don't want him needlessly worried.'

The man swallowed and nodded.

Turning his back on the stalled motorcade, Aarif headed into the swirling sand.

The wind was brisk, stinging what little of his face was still unprotected, but Aarif knew it could—would—get much worse. In another hour or two, the visibility would be zero, the winds well over a hundred miles an hour and deadly.

Deadly to Kalila, deadly to him. It was the princess he cared about; his own life he'd long ago determined was worthless. Yet if he failed to bring the princess back to Calista, if she died in his care…

Aarif squinted into the distance, refusing to let that thought, that fear creep into his brain and swallow his reason. He needed all his wits about him now.

The old horse balked at the unfamiliar terrain. She was a city animal, used to plodding ancient thoroughfares before heading home to her stable and bag of oats every night. The unforgiving wind and rocky ground were terrifying to her, and she let it be known with every straining step.

Aarif had always been kind to animals; it was man's sacred duty to provide for the beasts in his care, yet now his gloved hands clenched impatiently on the reins, and he fought the urge to scream at the animal, as if she could understand, as if that would help. As if anything would.

Where was Kalila? He forced himself to think rationally. She'd had a horse hidden behind the rocks, so someone had clearly helped her. She'd had a plan, a premeditated plan. The thought caused fresh rage to slice cleanly through him, but he pushed it away with grim resolution. He needed to think.

If she had a horse, she undoubtedly had some provisions. Not many, perhaps not more than he had, a bit of food, some water, a blanket. She was not an unintelligent woman, quite the contrary, so she must have a destination in mind, he reasoned. A safe place to shelter out the storm she knew about, the storm he'd *told* her about.

But where?

He drew the horse to a halt, scanning the horizon once more. Through the swirling sand he could just barely see the outlines of rocks, dunes, the ever-shifting shape of the desert. Nothing seemed like a probable resting place, yet he knew he would investigate every lone rock, every sheltered dune. It was his duty.

His duty. He wouldn't fail his duty; he'd been telling himself that for years, yet now, starkly, Aarif wondered when he *hadn't* failed. He shrugged impatiently, hating the weakness of his own melancholy, yet even now the memories sucked him under, taunted him viciously.

If you hadn't gone…if you hadn't said Zafir could come along…if you hadn't slipped…

If. If. If. Damnable, dangerous ifs, would-have-beens that never existed, never happened, yet they taunted him still, always.

If…your brother would still be alive.

Aarif swore aloud, the words torn from his throat, lost on the wind. The horse neighed pitifully, pushed already beyond her limited endurance.

And then he saw it. A dark grey speck on the horizon, darker than the swirling sand, the clouds. Rock. Many rocks, clustered together, providing safety and shelter, more so than anywhere else he could see. He knew, knew deep in his gut, that Kalila was making her way towards those rocks. Perhaps she was already there; she must have known the way.

He imagined her setting up her little camp, thinking herself safe, smiling to herself that she'd fooled them all, fooled *him*, played with their lives, with his own responsibilities and code of *honour*—

Cursing again, Aarif raised the reins and headed for the horizon.

She hadn't ridden so fast or furiously in months, years perhaps, and every muscle in Kalila's body ached. Her mind and heart ached too, throbbed with a desperate misery that made her wonder why she'd ever taken this stupid, selfish risk. She pushed the thought away; she couldn't afford doubt now. She couldn't afford pity.

Aarif had been right. A storm was blowing, a sirocco, the wet winds of the Mediterranean clashing with the desert's dry heat in an unholy cacophony of sound and fury. She had, Kalila guessed, maybe half an hour to set up shelter and get herself and her horse secure.

She murmured soothing endearments to her mare, As Sabr, and led her to where the huge boulder created a natural overhang, the small space under the shadow of stone enough for a tent, a horse.

Her father had taken her camping here when she was child; it was a no more than twelve kilo-metres from the palace, less even from Makaris, yet with the blowing sands it might have been a hundred.

Kalila set about her tasks, mindless, necessary. The tent was basic, with room only for two people.

Two people. Kalila's mind snagged and then froze on the thought, the realisation. If Aarif came after her…if he found her…

But, no. He had no idea where she was going, had never been in this desert before, didn't know the terrain, if he was out here at all. Surely in this storm he would turn back, he would wait. Any sensible man would do so, and yet…

Aarif did not seem a sensible man. He seemed, Kalila realised, remembering that hard look in his eyes, her heart beating sickly, a determined man.

What would she do if he found her? What would he do?

She pushed the thought, as she had a host of others, firmly away. No time to wonder, to fear. Now was the time for action only.

With the wind blowing more ferociously every second, it took Kalila longer to assemble the tent. She was furious with her own ineptitude, her soft hands and drumming heart. She'd assembled a tent like this—this tent even—a dozen, twenty times, yet now everything conspired against her; her hands cramped and slipped, her muscles ached, even her bones did. Her eyes stung and her mouth was desperately dry. Her heart throbbed.

Finally the tent was assembled and she took the saddlebags from As Sabr—food, blankets, water— and shoved them inside. She covered the horse with a blanket, drawing her closer against the rock for safety.

Then she turned to make her way into the tent, and her heart stopped. Her mouth dropped open. For there, only ten metres away, was a man. He was turbaned, robed, veiled except for his eyes, as she had been yesterday. He looked like a mythical creature, a hero—or perhaps a villain—from a fairy tale, an Arabian one.

It was, Kalila knew, Aarif.

He had found her.

Her mind froze, and so did her body. Kalila stood there, the winds buffeting her, the sand stinging her eyes, flying into her open mouth. She closed it, tasted grit, and wondered what would happen now. Her mind was beginning to thaw, and with it came a fearful flood of realisations, implications. Aarif looked furious. Yet with the realisation of his own anger was her own, treacherous sense of relief.

He had come.

Had she actually wanted him to find her? She was ashamed by the secret manipulations of her own heart, and she pushed the thought away as Aarif slid off his horse, leading the pathetic animal towards the shelter of the rock. His body was swathed in cloth, and she could only see his eyes, those dark, gleaming, angry eyes.

Kalila swallowed; more grit. Aarif came closer, the horse stumbling and neighing piteously behind him. Kalila still didn't move. Where could she go? She'd already run away and he'd found her. He'd found her so very easily.

He dealt with the animal first. From the corner of her eye Kalila saw him soothe the horse, give her water and a feed bag. He patted her down with a blanket, his movements steady, assured, yet Kalila could see the taut fury in every line of his body; she could feel it in the air, humming and vibrating between them with the same electricity that fired the storm.

The horse dealt with, he turned, and his gaze levelled her, decimated her. She swallowed again, choking on sand, and forced herself to keep his gaze, even to challenge it. Yet after a long moment she couldn't, and her gaze skittered nervously away.

The wind whistled around them with a high-pitched scream; in half an hour, less perhaps, the storm would be at its worst, yet still neither of them moved.

'Look at me,' Aarif said. His voice was low, throbbing, yet even with the shrieking wind Kalila heard it; she felt its demand deep in her bones, and she looked up.

Their eyes met, fought, and Kalila felt the onslaught of his accusation, his judgment. Aarif stared at her for a full minute, the dark fury of his gaze so much more than a glare, so much worse than anything she'd ever imagined.

She'd been so stupid.

And he knew. She knew.

Aarif muttered something—an expletive—and then in two quick strides he was in front of her, one hand stealing around her arm, the movement one of anger yet control.

'What were you thinking, Princess?' he demanded. His voice was muffled by the cloth over his face and he yanked it down. Kalila saw sand dusting his cheeks, his lips, his stubble. She swallowed again, desperate for water, for air. 'What were you thinking?' he demanded again, his voice raw, 'to come out here in a storm like this? To run away like a naughty child?' He threw one contemptuous arm towards the tent. 'Are you playing house, Princess? Is life nothing but a game to you?' His voice lowered to a deadly, damning pitch. 'Did you even think of the risk to you, to me, to our countries?'

Kalila lifted her head and tried to jerk her arm away, but Aarif held fast, his grip strong and sure. 'Let go of me,' she said. She would keep her pride, her defiance now; it was all she had.

He dropped her arm, thrust it away from him as if she disgusted him. Perhaps she did.

'You have no idea,' he said, and there was loathing and contempt in his voice, so great and deep and unrelenting that Kalila felt herself recoil in shame. 'No idea,' he repeated, shaking his head. 'And I thought you had.'

'You have no idea,' Kalila shot back. 'No idea what has gone on in my head, my heart—'

'I don't care,' he snarled and she jerked back proudly.

'No, of course not. So why ask what I was thinking? You've condemned me already.'

His gaze raked her and Kalila kept her shoulders back, her spine straight. She wouldn't cower now.

'Maybe I have,' Aarif said.

Another piercing shriek of wind, and then a louder, more horrifying crack. Aarif glanced up but before Kalila's mind could even process what she heard he'd thrust her back against the rock, her back pressed against the uneven stone, his body hard against hers.

The rock above them had broken off, a stress fracture in the stone that had finally given way in the wind, and fallen below with a sickening thud. Kalila swallowed. That could have—would have—fallen on her if Aarif had not pushed her out of the way.

She looked back at Aarif, and with a jolt of alarmed awareness she realised how close he was, his face inches from hers. His eyes bored into hers, his gaze so dark and compelling, yet with a strange, desperate urgency that caused an answering need to uncoil in her own belly.

His eyes searched her mind, her soul, and what did he find? What did he see? What did she want him to see?

She was suddenly conscious of his heart beating against hers, an unsteady rhythm, a staccato symphony of life. And with a knowledge of his heartbeat came another, more intimate awareness of his body pressed against hers. Even through the layers of dusty cloth she could feel the taut length of his torso, his thighs, his—

She gasped aloud, and with a curse Aarif jerked away as if she'd scorched him. Kalila stood there, her back still hard against the rock, stunned by her new knowledge.

Aarif had desired her.

'It is not safe out here,' he said brusquely, his eyes not meeting hers. 'You must go into the tent.'

Kalila nodded, her mind still spinning with this

new, surprising knowledge. Even facing the bleak prospects of her future, she had no desire to be left for dead in the desert, pinned by a fallen boulder.

She opened the tent flap and struggled in, only to realise after a prolonged moment that Aarif was not coming in with her.

He'd strode towards the horses, and, squinting, she could see him crouched on his haunches in the Eastern style between their lathered bodies, his back against the rock, his expression undeniably grim.

Exasperation, relief, and disappointment all warred within her. Of course a man like Aarif wouldn't want to share the cramped intimacy of the tent. Of course he would stoically insist on weathering a sandstorm outside, with the horses for company. It almost—almost—made her want to laugh.

But then she remembered the feel of his body against hers, the betrayal of his own instinct, as well as her answering need, and she pressed her hands to her hot cheeks.

Desire. It was a strange, novel thought. She hadn't felt desire for anyone; not what she thought of as desire, that inexorable tug of longing for another person. She'd never been close enough to another person to feel that yearning sweetness. Even in her years of freedom in Cambridge, she'd known she must be set apart. A princess had to be pure.

Yet in that moment, feeling the evidence of his

own desire and need, she'd felt an answering longing for Aarif and it had been as sweet, as sensuous a pleasure as a drug. It had uncoiled in her belly and spiralled upwards like warm wine through her veins, until all she'd been aware of was him.

Him.

It was the same feeling she'd felt at dinner, in the garden… since she'd met him. She just hadn't recognised it, because she'd never felt it before. Yet now it was so apparent, so obvious, what that feeling was. That hunger, that need. She knew enough about nature and humanity to recognise what Aarif had felt for her moments ago, and she understood the physical reaction of his body—and hers. She might be innocent, but she was not a child.

She did not feel like one.

She took a deep breath; it hurt her lungs. She needed water. Kalila scrabbled through the saddle-bags for her canteen, taking only a few careful sips to ease the raw parching of her throat.

Another breath and reason began to return. It had been a heated moment, she acknowledged, a moment of passionate anger. That was all it could be, what it had to be. It wasn't real; she didn't think Aarif even liked her. At least, he certainly didn't after what she'd done today.

She wasn't even sure she liked herself.

Kalila peered out of the tent flap. Even though Aarif was only a few metres away she could barely see him. Sighing in exasperation, she struggled out of the tent and stumbled in the near-darkness towards Aarif.

'You shouldn't be out here.'

'I've experienced worse, Princess,' Aarif told her flatly. He sat crouched on his haunches, his arms crossed. 'Go back in the tent where you belong.'

'You know the desert as well as I do,' Kalila returned. 'It is foolish to wait out here, not to mention dangerous. Why do you think I brought a tent?'

'I can only assume,' Aarif returned, his voice still tight with suppressed fury, 'that you had been planning your little escapade for some time.'

Kalila sighed, then sat down. 'Not as long as you think. If you're going to stay out here, then I am too, and it's likely the tent will blow away.'

She folded her arms, squinting to see him, the wind whipping her hair in tangles around her face. Aarif was silent, and Kalila waited, determined to win this battle of wills.

It was incredibly uncomfortable, though; the ground was hard, the wind merciless, the sand stinging every bit of exposed skin, and Aarif's glare was the harshest element of all. Still, she waited.

'You are the most stubborn woman I have ever met,' he said at last, and, though it wasn't a compliment, not remotely, Kalila smiled.

'I'm pleased you're beginning to realise that.'

A long moment passed as the wind shrieked around them. Muttering something—Kalila couldn't quite hear—Aarif rose fluidly from the ground and fetched his own saddlebags. 'Come, then,' he said, his voice taut. 'I will not risk your own foolish life simply because you choose to be so stubborn.'

Kalila rose, and his arm went around her shoulders, a heavy, strangely comforting weight, as he guided her back to the tent. They crawled through the flap in an inelegant tangle of limbs, half-falling into the small space.

And it was small, Kalila realised with a thrill of alarm. It would be difficult to avoid touching each other.

Aarif turned back to the tent flap. 'We must find a way to secure this, or you will have half the Sahara in here by morning.'

'I have some duct tape,' Kalila said, and dug through her saddlebags to find it.

He slotted her a thoughtful glance as she handed him the tape, although his eyes were still hard and unforgiving. 'You came prepared.'

She shrugged. 'I've camped in the desert many times. I simply knew what to bring.'

Aarif began to tape the flap shut, and it occurred to Kalila that they were locked inside. Trapped. Of course, she could remove the tape easily enough, but it still gave her the odd feeling of being in a prison cell, and Aarif was her jailor.

He turned to her, his eyes sweeping her with critical bluntness. 'You are a mess.'

'So are you,' she snapped, but she was instantly aware of her tangled hair, the sand embedded into her scalp.

'I imagine I am,' Aarif returned dryly. 'I was not prepared to go haring off into the desert in the middle of a sandstorm.' He shook his head, and when he spoke his voice was resigned. 'I don't know whether to think you a fool or a mad-woman.'

'Desperate,' Kalila told him flatly, and then looked away. The silence stretched between them, and she raked her fingers through the tangles in her hair, needing to be busy. She felt Aarif's eyes on her as she began to unsnarl the tangles one by one.

'Is marriage so abhorrent to you?' he asked eventually.

'Marriage to a stranger, yes,' Kalila replied, still not looking at him.

Aarif shook his head; she saw the weary movement out of the corner of her eye. 'Yet you knew you would marry my brother since you were twelve. Why choose your escape now, and such a foolhardy one?'

'Because I didn't realise how it would feel,' Kalila said, her voice low. She pulled her fingers through her hair again, attacking the tangles with a viciousness that she felt in her soul, her heart. 'When it came to the actual moment, when I thought Zakari would be there—'

Aarif exhaled, a sound of derisive impatience. 'Is this all simply because he did not come to fetch you? Your feelings are hurt too easily, Princess.'

Kalila swung her head around to meet his gaze directly. 'Perhaps, but yesterday—it clarified everything for me. I'd been going along waiting, hoping, believing I would do my duty, and then— all of a sudden—' She shook her head slowly. 'I thought, well, maybe I won't.'

'The thought of a child,' Aarif replied. 'What did you think? That you would flee into the desert for the rest of your life, live with the Bedouin? Did you think no one would ever find you?'

'No,' Kalila admitted slowly. 'I knew someone would. And even if they didn't, I would have to go back.'

'Then what—?'

'I just wanted to be free,' she said simply, heard the stark honesty, the blatant need in her voice. 'For a moment, a day. I knew it wouldn't last.'

Aarif eyed her unsympathetically. Freedom, to him she supposed, was unimportant. Unnecessary. 'And do you know how much you put at risk for an afternoon's *freedom*?' he asked. 'If your father discovers it—if Zakari does—'

'There's been no harm done,' Kalila objected. 'We're safe.'

'For now,' Aarif replied darkly. 'All is uncertain.'

'You have a grim view of things,' she replied, lifting her chin, clinging to her defiance though he picked at it with every unfeeling word he spoke. 'When you found me in the church, you were the same. Do you always think the worst is going to happen, Aarif?'

He reached for the canteen from his own bag. 'It often does,' he told her and unscrewed the top. Kalila watched him drink; for some reason she found she could not tear her gaze away from the long brown column of his throat, the way his muscles moved as he drank. He finally lifted the canteen from his mouth and she saw the droplets of water on his lips, his chin, and still she could not look away. She gazed, helpless, fascinated.

Slowly her eyes moved upwards to meet his own locked gaze, saw the intensity of feeling there—what was it? Anger? Derision?

Desire.

The moment stretched between them, silent, expectant, and Kalila again remembered his body against hers, its hard contours pressed against her, demanding, knowing. She swallowed, knowing she must look away, she must act, if not demure, then at least dignified.

'We should eat,' she said, and the words sounded stilted, forced. 'You must be hungry.'

Aarif said nothing, and Kalila did not risk looking at him again, seeing that unfathomable darkness in his eyes. Her hands trembled as she reached for bread and cheese, breaking off a bit of each and handing it to Aarif.

He took it with murmured thanks, and they ate quietly, neither speaking, neither looking at the other.

Was she imagining the tension coiling in the room, a far more frightening force than the wind that howled and moaned outside, rattling the sides of the tent as if it would sweep the shelter, and them inside, all away?

No, she was not, at least not in herself. She had never been so aware of another human being, the sounds of him chewing, of the cloth stretching across his body, even his breathing. She'd never had such an insane, instinctive desire to touch someone, to know what his hair, his skin felt like. Would his stubble be rough under her fingers? Would his hair be soft?

Horrified yet fascinated by the train of her thoughts, Kalila forced down a dry lump of bread and finally spoke, breaking the taut silence. 'Haven't you ever felt like that?'

'Like what?' Aarif's tone wasn't unfriendly, but it was close to it.

She swallowed again. 'Wanting to be free, if just for a moment. Haven't you ever wanted to…escape?'

He was silent for so long Kalila wondered if he was going to answer. When he finally spoke, his voice was heavy with a dark finality that Kalila knew she couldn't question. Wouldn't.

'Perhaps, when I was a child,' he said. 'But I outgrew such childish desires, and so must you.'

Kalila said nothing. Yes, she knew running away had been a childish, desperate desire, a moment's insanity, perhaps, and yet it had felt so good to be out on the desert, alone, in charge of her destiny, if only for an hour…even with the churning fear and regret, it had been good.

For a moment, she had been free.

She wondered if Aarif could ever understand that.

'Besides,' he continued, still unsympathetic, 'you had your years in Cambridge to be free, if this *freedom* is so important to you. Do you think my brother will veil you and lock you in the women's quarters? He is a modern man, Princess.'

'Yesterday you called me Kalila,' she blurted, and his lips compressed into a hard line.

'Yesterday was not today,' he said flatly, and Kalila wondered what he meant. She almost asked him, but then she remembered again the feel of his body against hers, his eyes pleading urgently— angrily—with hers, and she thought perhaps it was better not to know. Safer, anyway.

'What will happen?' she asked instead, heard the unsteadiness in her voice. 'Where is everyone?'

'God willing, they are sheltered at the airport. The storm will not die down until morning, I should think. We will return then.' His voice was grim, determined, and Kalila knew what he was thinking.

'And how will you explain our absence?'

'How will you?' he challenged. 'What will you say to your nurse, Kalila? She believed you were unwell. What will you say to all the civil servants of your country who have sworn to give their lives to protect you? Will you talk about *freedom* to them?' His voice rang out, contemptuous, condemning, and Kalila closed her eyes.

'Don't. I know…' She drew a shaky breath. 'I know I acted foolishly. Selfishly. I *know*!' She swept the crumbs off her lap, suddenly restless, needing activity, needing the freedom she had so desperately craved. Tears stung her eyes as she realised the full depth of her situation, her mess. And she'd caused it. Everything, she thought miserably, was her fault.

'How did you arrange it?' Aarif asked after a moment. 'Who brought the horse? The provisions?'

Her eyes flew to his even as her mind replayed the frantic, whispered conversation with a stable-boy that morning. 'I don't want to tell you.'

He shrugged, no more than the arrogant lifting of one powerful shoulder. 'I could find out easily enough.'

She thought of the shy, young boy, how she'd determinedly twisted him around her little finger, and felt another hot rush of guilt. 'I don't want—that person—punished.'

'You are the one who should be punished,' Aarif returned harshly. 'Not some frightened servant girl—or was it a besotted stableboy? Either one too weak to disobey your bidding!'

More condemnation. They piled on her head, a crippling burden she had to bear alone.

'It hardly matters,' she whispered. 'You've as good as guessed anyway.' She raised her eyes to his, seeking mercy from the one person who was least likely to give it. 'But tell me this, Aarif. Was it really so terribly selfish, so unforgivable, to allow myself one day—one afternoon—of freedom, when the rest of my life is spoken for?'

Her question was like a penny being dropped into a fountain, sending ripples through the stillness. Ripples of awareness, of feeling.

Aarif said nothing, but Kalila thought she saw a softening in his glance, however small, and it compelled her to continue. 'I don't want an arranged marriage. I'm willing to go through with it, and I'll do my duty by Zakari. I'll do my best. But I want to be loved, Aarif, and I think that's a natural desire. Human beings were created for love. To love and be loved. And even if Zakari grows to love me—and that, I know, is only an if—it's not the same. We weren't able to choose. Your father and stepmother chose love, and so did my parents. Why can't I?'

Her question rang out in a helpless, desperate demand, one that Aarif did not answer. 'Your destiny lay elsewhere,' he replied after a moment, his voice expressionless. He looked away.

'My destiny,' Kalila repeated, unable to keep the scorn from her voice. Not even wanting to. 'A destiny shaped by my father and yours, not by me. I want to choose my own destiny, or at least believe it could be different.'

'We do not always have that choice, Kalila.' His voice was low, almost gentle, although he still did not look at her.

'And what about you?' Kalila forced herself to ask. 'Don't you want love? To love someone and be loved back?' She knew it was an impertinent question, an imprudent one. It hinted at shadowy thoughts, memories, desires, nudged them to the light. It was, she realised, her heart fluttering in anticipation of his response, a dangerous question.

Yet she wanted to know. She *needed* to know.

'It doesn't matter what I want,' Aarif finally said, and it was clear he was ending the conversation. 'It never has. What matters is how best I can serve my family and country.'

'You don't take your own desires into consideration at all?' Kalila pressed, and when his eyes met hers they were flat and hard.

'No.'

Kalila felt as if she'd touched on something darker, some hidden memory or regret that suddenly filled the small space of the tent with its poisonous presence.

Aarif busied himself taking off his boots and spreading his blanket as far away from her as he could.

'We should sleep. We will ride out as soon as the storm breaks.'

Nodding slowly, Kalila reached for her own blanket. Aarif lay on his side, his back to her, his body still and tense.

She spread her own blanket out, removing her boots, stretching out gingerly. If she so much as moved her arm it would brush against Aarif's back, and as much as she was tempted to feel the bunched muscle underneath his shirt—a desire that surprised her with its sudden, unexpected urgency—she pressed backwards instead.

The wind still whistled and shrieked shrilly, and the flapping of the tent's sides was a ceaseless sound. On the wind she heard the horses neighing and moving in animalistic anxiety.

Tomorrow she would be back in civilisation, in Calista. She would meet Zakari. And what would she say? How would she explain what she had done? And why?

Kalila closed her eyes, unwilling to consider

the impossible answers to those questions. Tomorrow, she determined miserably, would have to take care of itself.

Kalila had no idea how either of them could sleep in this situation, yet even so fatigue fell over her in a fog. Still, her body was too tense, too aware, too miserable to relax into sleep. She lay awake, listening to the wind and Aarif's steady breathing.

Had he actually managed to fall asleep? It wouldn't surprise her. He was a man of infinite, iron control. Sleep, like everything else, would follow his bidding.

Finally, after what felt like several hours, she fell into an uneasy doze, woken suddenly in the middle of the night.

All was dark and silent; the storm had abated and the stillness of the aftermath carried its own eerie tension. Yet there was a sound, a faint moaning, and Kalila wondered if it was the wind or one of the animals, still uneasy in the unfamiliar surroundings.

But no, she realised, the sound was coming from inside the tent. From right next to her, little more than a tortured breath, a whispered plea of anguish. She shifted, the blanket rustling underneath her, and squinted through the moonlit darkness.

Aarif lay on his back, the blanket twisted around him, a faint sheen of sweat glistening on his skin. His lips were parted in a grimace, his eyelids twitching as he battled his nightmare.

For surely it was a nightmare that held him in its grip, Kalila realised, for the sound, that piteous moan, was coming from Aarif.

CHAPTER FIVE

IT WAS the same, it was always the same. Agonisingly, torturously the same, where he could never change what had happened, what *would* happen, replaying again and again in his mind as he watched, helpless, hopeless…

He knew it was a dream, and still he could not wake himself from it. The nightmare grabbed him by the throat, swallowed him whole in its cavernous jaws, so all he could hear was his brother's choked cry of desperation.

'*Aarif…*'

And he did nothing. He felt the searing heat across his face once more, his hands reaching out to grasp—to save—his brother, but Zafir was too far, and farther still, his face pale and terrified as Aarif fell into the water and it rushed into his mouth and nose, closed over his head…

'Aarif…' The voice was softer, sweeter now, a whisper from another world, the real world, yet still the dream did not let him go. He shook from the force of it, great tremors that racked his body with emotional agony.

'Aarif…' It was Zafir again, his voice trailing away, the cry of a boy, a child, and yet holding the relentless ring of condemnation. 'Save me…'

The voice rang in his eyes, faint and desperate, and there was nothing Aarif could do. There was nothing he could ever do.

Aarif shifted restlessly on his blanket, his face contorted with both pain and anguish.

'Aarif…' Kalila whispered, but he didn't hear her. Couldn't. He was locked in a far more terrible world than the one they currently inhabited. Tentatively Kalila reached over to touch his shoulder, wanting to stir him into wakefulness, but Aarif jerked away from her light touch.

'No…*no*!' His desperate scream ripped through the stillness of the tent, the night, and caused Kalila's hand to freeze inches from his shoulder. That agonised shriek was a sound she would never forget. It was the sound of a man in mental agony, mortal pain.

Aarif let out another shuddering breath, his hands bunching on the blanket, and Kalila saw the faint, silvery tracks of tears on his cheeks.

Her heart twisted painfully at the sight of so much suffering. What kind of dream could hold him in such terrible captivity?

'Aarif…' she tried again, her voice stronger now. 'It's all right. It's just a dream.' Yet even as she spoke she realised it was not just a dream. A mere figment of imagination could not hold Aarif so strongly in its thrall. This was something far more terrible, far more real.

Kalila couldn't bear to see him suffering so; it cut at her heart and she felt near tears herself. She leaned over him, smoothing the damp hair away from his forehead. *'Aarif,'* she said again, her voice breaking, and then he opened his eyes.

Their faces were close, so close that when his eyes opened it felt as if he touched her with his gaze. Kalila was conscious of her hand still stroking his hair as if he were a child to be comforted.

Aarif stared at her, the vestiges of his private torment still visible on his ravaged face, and then he let out a choked cry and tried to roll away.

He couldn't; she wouldn't let him. She didn't know why she wouldn't, only that she acted on instinct. No one deserved to bear that kind of pain alone. 'Don't,' she whispered. Her fingers threaded through his hair, drawing his gaze back to hers. 'What torments you so?' she whispered. Aarif said nothing. She could feel his racing heart, heard him swallow back another cry. Gently, a movement born still of instinct, she trailed her fingers down his cheek, tracing the path of his scar as if her touch could heal that grim reminder of what—?

Kalila didn't even know, but she felt it, knew the pain Aarif was experiencing must be a personal memory, a private grief. His hand clamped over hers, his fingers trapping and yet clinging to hers, and he shook his head, trying to speak, but unable to.

Kalila stilled, her fingers on his face, and Aarif closed his eyes. A shudder went through his body, a tremor of remembered emotion, and naturally—too naturally—Kalila put her arms around him and drew him to herself.

His head was on her shoulder, his silky hair brushing her lips, his body, hard and muscular, against hers. His arms came around her, and Kalila realised she had never been so close to a man, every part of their bodies in intimate contact. It felt natural, right, this closeness, their bodies wrapped around each other in an embrace born of comfort and need. It humbled her that a man like Aarif would accept her caress, that he might even need it.

Neither of them spoke.

His still-racing heart pounded against her own chest, and after many long moments where the only sound was Aarif's ragged breathing she felt it slow. She stroked his hair, felt his fingers tighten reflexively on her shoulder. Still neither of them moved beyond those tiny gestures, neither of them spoke.

Kalila knew that to speak, to even think would break the moment between them, with its precious fragility, its tenuous tenderness. In a day and night of unreality, this felt real. It felt, she thought distantly, before her mind turned hazy and still once more, right.

Another long moment passed and Aarif's breathing steadied. Now was the time, Kalila knew, for them to roll away, to close their eyes, to forget this brief and wonderful intimacy, this moment of desire stolen from a lifetime of duty.

Yet she didn't, and she knew with a sudden, thrilling certainty that Aarif wouldn't. She knew as he lifted his head, his eyes gazing darkly, hungrily into hers, what he would do.

He kissed her.

It was not the hard, urgent kiss she'd been half expecting, something born of the reckless desperation of this stolen moment. Instead it was sweet, tentative, his mouth moving gently over hers until it bloomed into something stronger and sweeter still as he deepened the contact, his tongue exploring her lips, her mouth, his hands reaching to cup her face, to draw her even closer, as if he was seeking something from her—and she gave it.

Kalila gave herself up to that kiss, let it reverberate through her heart and mind, body and soul. It was, she thought hazily, a wonderful first kiss. For she'd never been kissed before, not like this, not like anything.

She'd kept herself apart, pure, as she'd always meant to do, as she'd had to do as a princess betrothed since she was twelve. Yet now her mind drifted away from that realisation, for with it came the ugly knowledge that this was far more wrong and selfish an act than running away in the first place.

This was betrayal of the deepest kind, yet her mind—and heart—skittered away from that word for this felt too wonderful. Too right.

The kiss deepened, lengthened and grew into hands and touch, their bodies a living map to be explored and understood.

Aarif fumbled at first with her clothes, but somehow the buttons and snaps gave way and her skin was bare to his fingers, his hands gliding over her flesh before his lips followed, and Kalila gasped at the intimacy, the exposure that made her feel vulnerable and yet treasured.

Loved.

They moved as one, in silence, the only sound a drawing of breath, a sigh of pleasure, the whispering slide of skin against skin. It felt like a dream, a wonderful and healing dream, as Aarif's hands moved over her, touching her in places that had known no man's caress.

She opened herself up to him, parting her legs, arching her back, wanting his touch, needing this new caress, this forbidden intimacy.

And then she touched him, tentatively at first, her hands exploring, seeking, discovering the hard, muscled plane of his chest and stomach, the surprisingly smooth curve of his hip, the ridges on his back—more scars.

Now was not the time to ask where they came from, what terrible memory Aarif kept locked in his heart. Now, Kalila thought, her lips touching the places her hands had gone, brushing over that satiny skin, was the time for healing.

She wouldn't think about what this meant. She pushed the thought, the implications, firmly away, and let herself drift in a haze of feeling and emotion, let Aarif's hands and mouth seek her as she gave herself up to him and the maelstrom of pleasure and wonder he caused to whirl within her.

She'd never imagined the feelings to be strong—sharp—she gasped as he touched her, gasped in surprise and wonder, and felt Aarif smile against her skin. She loved that she'd made him smile, that there was a joy to be found here.

And yet a moment came—as Kalila knew it would have to—when they could have stopped. Should have. Clothing bunched and pushed aside, their bodies bare and touching, Aarif moved on top of her, poised to join his body to hers in an act so intimate, so sacred and precious and unfamiliar, and yet so right. His eyes sought and met hers, a silent agreement. They gazed at each other, neither speaking, both complicit, and then their bodies joined as one.

Kalila gasped at the feeling, her hands bunching on his back, the twinge of discomfort lost in the exquisite sensation of this union, the fullness of him inside her, the sense of completion that reverberated through her body and heart.

Aarif buried his head in her shoulder, his hair brushing her lips, his body straining for both of their releases, and she clasped him to her, gasping in wonder and shock. She never wanted the moment to end, never wanted to feel alone again—

The realisation was as wonderful as the sensation of his body moving in hers, and as her body finally gave itself up to the spiralling pleasure and the joy she found that at last, now, she felt free. That she knew who she was.

What she'd been meant for.

The aftermath, she thought as Aarif rolled away from her, was as eerie and silent as that of the storm. Aarif lay on his back, one arm flung over his face. The silence that had wound its seductive spell around them moments before now stretched taut as a wire, and just as sharp.

Kalila was suddenly conscious of the sand in her scalp, the stickiness on her thighs. Moments before she'd felt only joy, and now it was replaced by something far worse. Something sordid. She felt used and cheap and dirty, and she didn't want to.

Yet, a whisper within her mocked, *isn't that just what you are? You just betrayed your fiancé with his brother.*

She closed her eyes, felt the flood of remorse that she'd kept at bay while pleasure had reigned in her body and heart, still turned her bones to runny wax. She felt the regret wash over her in engulfing waves, and could only imagine how Aarif felt.

Aarif…a man bound by duty and honour. A man with whom responsibility weighed heavily, endlessly. What could he be thinking now?

She sneaked a glance at him and saw he hadn't moved. Only moments ago she'd touched his skin, kissed him, *loved* him.

Love.

Could she love Aarif? *Did* she?

She barely knew him; he was unforgiving, unemotional, *unpleasant*, and yet when she'd held him in her arms…

When he'd touched her as if he knew her, not just her body, but her heart. Her mind.

When he'd smiled.

Kalila swallowed. She couldn't possibly love Aarif, yet what had happened between them was real, it was *something*—

'Aarif.' Her voice came out in a croak. She had no idea what to say, where to begin—

'Don't.' The one word was harsh, guttural, savage. Aarif rolled up in one fluid movement, his face averted from hers, and with a vicious jerk he peeled the tape away from the door. Kalila watched him, her heart starting to pound with a relentless anxiety, and a deep misery settled coldly in her bones.

Another jerk and the tape was off; he flung it to the floor before pushing through the flap and out into the desert's darkness.

Kalila could hear the crunch of his bare feet on the sand, the low nicker of one of the horses and Aarif's soothing murmur back. Tears—stupid tears—stung her eyes. He was kinder to the horses than he was to her.

And yet, that insistent whisper protested, *the horses didn't do anything. They are innocent. You are not.*

Innocence. So prized, so precious. So important for a woman like her, a woman poised to marry a king, and she was innocent no longer. Instinctively Kalila glanced down, saw a faint rusty smear of blood on her thigh. In another age that bit of blood would have been proof of her innocence, her purity, her whole reason for being a wife. It would have been displayed with bawdy jokes and satisfied smiles. In another age, she realised, swallowing down a hysterical laugh, she would have been killed for what she had just done.

Her innocence was gone.

And yet even so, despite the regret and shame and even fear coursing through her, she couldn't forget the feeling of Aarif in her arms, in her body. She couldn't forget, and she didn't want to.

What kind of woman did that make her?

She took a shuddering breath, tried to calm her racing thoughts, her racing heart. She needed to think, to plan. She needed to speak with Aarif.

With a bit of water from the canteen she cleaned herself up as best she could and dressed, combing the tangles from her hair with her fingers.

Then, taking another deep breath for courage, she slipped through the flap and out into the cool night.

The air was cold and sharp, the sky glittering with stars. The sand dunes were cast in silver by the moonlight, and the air after the storm was perfectly still.

Signs of devastation could be glimpsed, shadows of broken rocks, twisted roots. Briefly Kalila offered up a prayer for the rest of her party, sheltering at the airport. She prayed no one would lose a life because of her own folly.

Her own selfishness.

She moved gingerly across the sand to Aarif; his back was to her, one arm braced against the rock overhang. His head was bowed, every taut line of his body radiating anguish. Anger.

She stood a few metres behind him, her arms creeping around herself in the cold, and waited.

What could she say? What could he say?

What, she wondered distantly, could happen now?

A long moment of silence passed; the horses shifted fretfully and a slight breeze stirred the hair lying limply against her face. Then Aarif spoke.

'What we'll do,' he said in a cold, flat voice, as if they were in the middle of a conversation, 'is tell everyone I found you this morning. You sheltered here alone, and I found a protected place of my own. Then at least your reputation will not be called into question. I don't think there is anyone in the party who wishes to cast doubt on you or this marriage union.'

Kalila heard his words echoing relentlessly through her, but they didn't make sense. He was sticking a plaster on a wound that required major surgery.

'That's all very well,' she finally said when she'd found her voice, 'but it hardly addresses the real situation.'

'I hardly think you want your father's staff knowing what happened,' Aarif replied, his voice still cold and so horribly unemotional. 'I am trying to salvage this mess, Princess.'

'How? By lying?'

'By protecting you!' Aarif turned around, and Kalila took an instinctive step backwards at the anguished fury twisting his features. 'God knows I made this mess, and I will be the one to clean it up.'

He spoke with such a steely determination that Kalila quelled.

'How?' she whispered.

'I will have to tell Zakari.'

She closed her eyes, not wanting to imagine that conversation, or what it meant for her. For her marriage. 'Aarif, if you do that, you will ruin my marriage before it even begins.'

'I will tell Zakari that it is my fault—'

'And you think he will believe that? That you *raped* me?' She shook her head, disbelief and disappointment warring within her. She didn't want this, this sordid discussion of what had just happened between them. She couldn't bear to talk cold logistics when her heart cried out for him now—still—

'I was responsible,' Aarif insisted in a low voice. 'I should have stopped, turned away—' He shook his head. 'I accused you of being selfish, Kalila, but it is I who have been the most selfish of all.' He muttered something under his breath and stalked away, his body so taut his muscles almost seemed to be vibrating with a seething self-loathing.

Kalila took a few tentative steps towards him. She wanted to touch him, to reach him, yet every instinct told her she couldn't. He had shut himself off completely, walled himself with his own sense of responsibility and guilt.

Still, she tried.

'Aarif, I could have protested. I could have stopped. We are both to blame.' His back was to her, and he said nothing. Dragging a breath into her lungs, she forced herself to continue, to lay her heart open to him as her body had been. 'The truth is, I didn't want to. I wanted to be with you, Aarif, from the moment you touched me. The moment I touched you, for if we are going to apportion blame, then I was the one who first—'

'Don't,' he cut her off, 'romanticise what was nothing more than a bout of lust.'

Kalila blinked. She felt as if she had been slapped. Worse, she felt as if he'd taken the handful of memories they'd just created and crumpled them into a ball and spat on them. 'No,' she whispered, 'it wasn't.' Aarif was silent, and she spoke again, her voice wavering and then finally breaking, 'Aarif, don't make this into something sordid—'

'It is sordid!' he snapped. 'Everything about it is sordid, Kalila, can't you see that? My brother trusted me, *trusted* me, with your care. He asked me to come fetch you because he believed he could depend on me, and I did the worst thing—the only thing—that would betray him utterly.' He swivelled to face her, his face pitilessly blank. 'There is nothing good about what happened, Kalila. Not one thing. You might have felt a brief pleasure in my

arms, but it was cheap and worthless, and if you had
any sense of honour or duty, you would know it.'

Kalila opened her mouth but she couldn't think
of a single thing she could say. Tears rolled slowly,
coldly, down her cheeks. Aarif watched her with
such an obvious lack of sympathy that she felt as
vulnerable and exposed as she had underneath him,
her body open to his caress.

'I know what you're thinking,' he said, his voice
as sharp and cutting as a razor. 'You're thinking
you've fallen in love with me.' He spoke the
word—love—with such contempt that Kalila
could only blink. 'You told me you wanted love.
Not an arranged marriage, you said. And so now
you think this is it. Love.' He shook his head,
holding up one hand to stop her from speaking,
although Kalila's mind was too shocked and numb
to frame even a syllable. 'Oh, I don't think you
realised what you were doing. You were caught up
in the moment as much as I was, but now you're
desperate to make it into something, to believe we
have something.' He spoke with a sneer that reverberated through her. 'Well, we don't, Princess. All
we have is a mistake, and it is my duty to rectify
it. As for your marriage—Zakari is a kind man. He
can forgive.' He paused, his lip curling. 'He'll have
to.' He turned to walk away, to leave her alone
with his harsh words, his cold condemnation.

Kalila's head was bowed under the weight of his

judgment, and she spoke through stiff lips. 'You are saying this because it's the only way you can accept what happened.'

Aarif stilled, stiffened. 'Still clinging to fairy tales?' he mocked, but she heard—hoped she heard—a current of deeper hurt and even need beneath his sneering tone.

'This doesn't feel like much of a fairy tale to me,' Kalila replied, lifting her head, her chin tilted at a proud, defiant angle. 'I'm not going to cheapen what happened between us, Aarif, simply because it was wrong. And, yes, I know it was wrong. I accept that, but I also accept that for a few moments you clung to me, you needed me, and I needed you. And we found something together that I can't believe everyone finds.' Tears sparkled on her lashes, she felt another one drip onto her cheek, but she kept his gaze. 'Believe what you want, if it makes you feel better,' she said. 'Believe your own version of the fairy tale, Aarif, but I know the truth.'

Aarif's mouth tightened in a hard line, his eyes dark and angry. Kalila looked up and saw the stars were fading into an eerie grey dawn, the first pale pink finger of daybreak lighting the flat horizon. 'It's morning,' she said. 'Time to go.'

They packed up in stiff silence. Kalila wrapped herself in numbness; the pain and the realisation, the repercussions and the bittersweet memories, could all come later. They would come, she knew; she wouldn't be able to stop them.

For now, she busied herself with mundane tasks of rolling blankets and folding the tent, feeding the animals and making herself as presentable as she could given their limited resources.

She had no mirror, but she didn't need one to know her hair was in a wild tangle, her eyes dry and gritty, her face wind-reddened, her hands rough and chapped.

Would Zakari be waiting at the Calistan airport? Would he see her like this?

Would he *know*?

For the first time she hoped he was still seeking after his precious diamonds. The longer he stayed away, the longer the reprieve she had. The longer until the reckoning.

And yet it would come. She knew it would come, and the thought had the power to dry the breath in her lungs and cause her heart to pound with relentless anxiety until she surrounded herself in numbness once more.

It took them three hours to ride to the airport. Kalila was weary and saddle sore, conscious of the new tenderness between her thighs, the utter, aching weariness in every muscle, sinew and bone.

She followed behind Aarif as the sun rose higher in the sky, its rays merciless and punishing. Aarif did not falter once as they made their way through the shifted sand, a landscape utterly changed from yesterday, and yet he rode with an unerring sense of direction, of rightness.

Of course, Kalila thought with a weary wryness, of course he would know just how to get to the airport, an airport he'd never even been to. A man like Aarif never strayed off the path, never made a wrong turn—

Except once. Last night he had.

What had caused him to stumble? To reach out for someone, for her? Kalila's heart ached as she thought of it, remembered how it felt to hold Aarif, to be held by him. To be needed, touched, loved.

You're thinking you've fallen in love with me.

Her mouth compressing into a grim line, Kalila lowered her head and focused on the rough trail, her mare plodding wearily after Aarif's mount.

When the airport, a low, humble building of tin and concrete, came into view, Kalila almost felt relieved. She was tired of the waiting, the tension. She wanted to get it over with, the explanations, the lies. Then she wanted a hot bath.

Juhanah came running out first, her face grey with anxiety. 'Oh, *ya daanaya*! My child! We feared you were dead, both of you!' Even as Juhanah wrapped her in an embrace the old nurse's eyes slid speculatively to Aarif and Kalila saw it.

So it begins, she thought, closing her eyes and letting herself be comforted. The whispers, the rumours. Her reputation couldn't be protected, not from imaginations, minds.

And it didn't even deserve to be.

'I found Princess Kalila a few hours ago,' Aarif said. He'd slid off the horse and handed the reins to an aide, giving terse instructions for both horses to be returned. 'She'd taken shelter in the storm, as I had, and when the winds died down I came upon where she had been waiting out the storm.' He spoke coolly, impersonally, his gaze flicking not even once to her. And stupidly, irrationally, Kalila felt hurt.

She almost started to believe the terrible things he'd said to her that morning.

'Thank God,' Juhanah said, clutching Kalila to her bosom once more. 'Thank God you found her, Prince Aarif.' She took Kalila by the shoulders, giving her a little shake as if she were still an unruly child to be disciplined. 'What were you thinking, Kalila? To run off like that? If your father had discovered—'

'King Bahir does not need to know about a young woman's moment of foolishness,' Aarif cut in smoothly. His voice was pleasant although there was a warning hardness to his eyes. 'The princess explained to me that she had a moment of folly, of fear. It is a fearsome thing, for a young woman to meet a husband she has never seen. For a moment—a moment only—the princess thought to run away. She did not go far, and in truth she was planning to turn around when the storms caught her. She knew she wouldn't make it back to the caravan, so she sheltered by a rock. I found her in the morning, and we returned at once.' Aarif smiled, this recitation of lies so easily given that even Kalila was almost convinced, despite the obvious evidence to the contrary. Yet if anyone thought of it, no one dared to ask why her mare, As Sabr, was there with saddlebags and provisions.

It would be better for everyone, Kalila acknowledged, to pretend this hadn't happened. Unfortunately, she wasn't sure she could do that. Her glance slid to Aarif, but he wasn't looking at her. His face was hard, blank, resolute, and Kalila wondered if she would ever see the other side of him again.

Conscious of an uncomfortable silence and the many pairs of staring eyes, she forced herself to give a weak nod before bowing her head. 'It is true, Juhanah. I had a moment of weakness, and I regret it deeply. It was wrong of me.' Her head still bowed, her gaze slid once more to Aarif—wanting something from him, even now—but he was staring fixedly ahead, a cool and remote look on his face even though he smiled.

'Poor darling,' Juhanah murmured. 'At least no one has been harmed.'

'Everyone sheltered safely here?' Aarif surmised, and when this was confirmed he gave a brisk nod and moved towards the airport, already taking out his mobile and punching in some numbers. 'Then it is time to return to Calista.'

Juhanah made a squeak of protest. 'But Prince Aarif! The princess is tired and dirty. She cannot meet her intended this way. We must return to the palace so she can wash, prepare—'

Aarif turned around. 'I fear that would not be wise, madam. The princess's place is in Calista now. As for the king seeing her in disarray, never fear.' He held up his mobile. 'I have just received a message that he has been delayed, so there will be time for the princess to prepare herself—' he glanced at Kalila, who jerked under his cool gaze '—as she sees fit.'

With a little nod, Aarif turned and walked into the airport.

'Poor darling,' Juhanah fussed again. 'To not even bathe or change your clothes—'

'There is a washroom in the airport,' Kalila said with a shrug. She didn't want Juhanah's motherly fussing, didn't deserve it. 'I'll wash my face and comb my hair and be myself in no time.'

Yet the words held a hollow ring, for Kalila knew she would not be herself again. She'd found herself—her freedom—in Aarif's embrace, and she was unlikely to do so ever again.

CHAPTER SIX

THE plane left the barren desert of Zaraq to glide over a smooth expanse of jewel-toned sea, the sky cloudless, blue, and perfect, the water calmed after the storm that had ravaged both land and sea in its ferocious grip.

Kalila leaned her head against the window and feigned sleep. She was weary—exhausted—yet the sanctuary of sleep eluded her. Still, she wished to avoid questions, and next to her Juhanah seemed poised to ask them.

Only Juhanah, herself, and Aarif were on the plane, as the other staff had returned to the palace with their own version of events. Kalila wondered what her father would think of her mad escape, yet even the thought of his anger failed to rouse her from her numb lethargy. She was beyond his reach now. The person to fear now was Zakari, and yet she couldn't quite summon the energy. He was not in Calista yet; she was safe. For a while.

Once she glanced back at Aarif, seated in a deep leather seat behind her, papers spread out on his lap. A pair of spectacles perched on his aquiline nose, and for some reason that little sign of human frailty touched her, made her remember the man who had reached out to her, who had buried his head in her shoulder. The man who had needed her.

Juhanah glanced at her, sharply, and Kalila realised she'd let her gaze linger too long. She turned back to the window and was about to close her eyes again when a stretch of land—desert once more—came into view.

Calista.

Her home.

Kalila craned her neck to take it in, the stretch of sand so similar to Zaraq, the winding blue-green of a river, twisting through rocky hills, where she knew Calista's famous diamonds were mined. Then, the Old Town, similar to Makaris yet somehow imposing in its unfamiliarity. She glimpsed a huddle of buildings, flat roofed, with a wide market square in the middle.

And finally, the palace. Made of a similar mellow, golden stone as the Zaraquan palace, its simple and elegant design speaking of centuries of rule, of royalty.

The plane glided past the palace and approached the airport, and Kalila sat back in her seat once more.

Aarif did not speak to her as they disembarked

from the plane. A black sedan from the palace met them and again Aarif avoided her, sitting in the front with the driver while she and Juhanah shared the back.

Kalila was barely aware of the passing scenery, more desert, scattered palm trees, and then, closer to the city, the island's polo club, and the newer part of town with a sign for Jaladhar, the island's resort.

Exhaustion, emotional and physical, was crashing over her in wave after merciless wave and all she wanted was to sleep. To forget…if only for a few minutes or hours.

The car pulled up to the palace on the edge of the Old Town, and a servant dressed in official livery came out to greet them. The man's bland expression faltered for a moment as he took in Kalila's appearance, for, though she'd repaired some of the damage, she was hardly the royal presence he'd expected.

She smiled and he swept a bow, launching into a formal speech of obsequious flattery that Kalila barely registered.

'The Princess Kalila is much fatigued,' Aarif said, not looking at her, and the servant straightened. 'Please show her and her nurse to their rooms and afford them every comfort.'

And then, without a backward glance, he swept into the palace. Kalila watched his back disappear behind the ornate wooden doors and wondered when she would see him again. She had a feeling that Aarif would make every effort to avoid her.

She followed the servant into the palace, and a waiting maid led them up a sweeping staircase to the second floor, a narrow corridor of ancient stone with open windows, their Moorish arches framing a view of azure sky and endless sand.

Although the palace was situated in the island's main city, Serapolis, on the edge of the Old Town, the women's quarters faced the private gardens, a verdant oasis much like the one back in Zaraq, although, Kalila reflected from the window of her bedroom, not as familiar.

Everything was strange. Even she felt strange, a stranger to herself. She'd acted in ways she'd never imagined herself acting in the last twenty-four hours, and she had no idea what the repercussions would be, only that they would be severe and long lasting.

She sighed, a sound that came from the depths of her soul, and Juhanah looked at her in concern. 'You must be tired. Let me run you a bath.'

Kalila nodded, grateful for her nurse's tender concern. 'Thank you, Juhanah.'

While Juhanah padded into the en suite bathroom, Kalila glanced around the bedroom that had been assigned her. It was a simple room, yet no less sumptuous for it. A wide bed with a white linen duvet, a cedar chest at its foot. A matching bureau and framed mirror, and two arched windows that framed the view of the gardens outside.

A few minutes later Kalila entered the bathroom, outfitted with every luxury from the sunken marble tub to the thick, fluffy towels, and sank into the hot, foaming water with a little sigh of relief. From behind the closed door she could hear Juhanah moving around, and realised her bags had arrived.

It felt good to wash the dirt and sand away, yet no amount of washing would make her feel clean again. Whole. Even now a pall of misery settled over her, into her bones, so that she wondered numbly if she would ever be apart from it—be herself—again.

Yet who was she? Caught between two worlds, two lives, two dreams. Duty. Desire. It had only been in Aarif's arms, under his caress, that she'd felt whole. One. With him.

Juhanah knocked on the door. 'All right, *ya daanaya*?'

'Yes, I'm fine,' she called. Her nurse's maternal worrying was sweet, yet it also made Kalila feel guilty. She didn't deserve Juhanah's concern. What would her nurse say if she told her…?

Kalila closed her eyes. She wouldn't tell her, wouldn't tell anyone. And yet Aarif would tell someone. He'd said as much. He would tell his brother.

What had she been expecting to happen? she wondered. Had she thought Aarif would tell her he loved her, that everything had changed? Had she actually believed, even for a moment, that an hour or two of passion changed everything? Anything?

Yet it had seemed so much more than that. When she'd held him in her arms, felt his heart beating against hers, felt that they were *one*…

That was what she wanted, she realised. That was why her heart and mind resisted marriage to Calista's king. She wanted love, and for a few moments it had felt as if she'd found it with Aarif.

You're thinking you've fallen in love with me. His words that morning mocked her. How could she believe it was love when she barely knew him? And what she knew, she wasn't entirely sure she liked.

He was hard, unrelenting, grim-faced, determined. Yet she'd seen flickers of humour, tenderness, need.

No, she didn't love him, Kalila knew. Yet she wondered if she *could*.

She also wondered about the dream that had tormented him so, what horrible memory still held him in its grip. Understanding that memory, Kalila felt, would be a key to understanding Aarif.

Yet how could she understand him when he would spend the next few weeks avoiding her at all costs? And, she reminded herself bleakly, when she was still engaged to his brother?

The water had grown cold and Kalila soaped herself quickly, her hands suddenly stilling on her flat belly. Yet another repercussion of those few moments with Aarif occurred to her with icy shock.

Pregnancy. A baby.

Aarif's child.

Yet even as her lips curved in a helpless smile at that thought, her mind recognised the disastrous consequences of such a possibility. A royal bastard, conceived before she'd even been married.

Of course, Kalila knew, Zakari could think the baby was his, conceived on their still-to-be wedding night, but if Aarif told him—

She closed her eyes again. This was such a mess. A mess, a mistake, and she had no idea how to fix it or where to begin. She thrust the thoughts away, all of them, to untangle later. It was too much to deal with now, and Kalila had a feeling it would *always* be too much.

The bath had made her sleepy, and when Kalila emerged from the bathroom swathed in a robe and saw the wide, comfortable bed with the duvet turned down, it seemed only natural to slip between the crisp, clean sheets and let herself be lulled to sleep by the lazy whirring of the ceiling fan. The last sound she heard was the gentle click of the door as Juhanah let herself out.

When she awoke to the sound of a knock on the

door, the sun was low in the sky, the room cast in shadow, the air sultry and still. Kalila pushed the hair out of her eyes and called, 'Juhanah?'

'Yes, Princess,' Juhanah replied, and entered. Kalila watched her nurse bustle around the room, a fixed smile on her face, yet something had clearly ruffled her.

Kalila sat up in bed. 'What time is it?'

'Past five o'clock,' Juhanah replied.

'When are we to dine?'

Juhanah pursed her lips briefly before replying, 'Prince Aarif has suggested we eat privately tonight, here in your rooms. He said the journey will have fatigued you too much to bear a formal meal.'

Kalila's lips twitched at Juhanah's barely disguised expression of outrage at this perceived slight. 'How very thoughtful of him,' she said dryly, knowing full well why Aarif would issue such a suggestion.

'Indeed,' Juhanah agreed huffily, 'although hardly a fitting reception for a royal princess!'

Kalila shrugged. 'I don't—'

'Of course you don't mind,' Juhanah cut her off, clearly too outraged to let her complaints go unspoken. 'You are young and easily pleased. But I do not know what to think of a palace that is shut up like a box with no one inside, no one to greet you but a lowly servant—'

'Actually, he looked quite important—'

'Pfft!' Juhanah made a dismissive gesture with her hand. 'It is not right.'

'You must remember there has been a great deal of upheaval in the royal family,' Kalila replied, the words as much a reminder to herself as to Juhanah. 'With King Aegeus of Aristo dying, and the rumours of the missing diamond—'

'And is that where they all are? On a wild goose chase for some jewel?' Hands on hips, Juhanah looked thoroughly disgruntled, and Kalila found herself smiling, her heart suddenly, surprisingly light.

She rose to embrace her nurse, who returned the hug with some surprise. Kalila had never been an overly affectionate child, yet now she felt a rush of gratitude, a need for touch. 'I'm glad you're here, Juhanah,' she said. 'I don't think I could bear this all alone.'

Juhanah patted her head, stroking the tangled curls. 'And you shouldn't have to. I shall stay in Calista as long as you want me, *ya daanaya.*'

'Thank you,' Kalila whispered, and felt a sudden wave of homesickness, followed by the sting of unexpected tears. She choked them both back down and moved away. 'Even if we're dining right here, I should dress,' she said, and opened the bureau where Juhanah had already put away her clothes.

A short while later a servant wheeled in a domed trolley with a three-course meal set on porcelain plates. Even if most of the royal family was not in residence, the cook clearly was and after twenty-four hours of riding rations Kalila was grateful for the rich offerings: sweet peppers stuffed with lamb, a tangine of chickpeas and tomatoes, and semolina cakes made with dates and cinnamon.

After the meal had been cleared away, Kalila told Juhanah she was sleepy again and the nurse retired to her own room.

Yet sleep, for now, eluded her. Outside her window the moon hung like a silver sickle in the sky, and the gardens beckoned, fragrant and cool. Kalila thought of stealing out there, wandering along the winding stone paths, but she decided against it. The garden could be explored in the light of day.

Yet she refused to be shut up in her room like a prisoner. Aarif might prefer it, but at this point Kalila was not inclined to make things easier for him.

She checked her appearance in the wide mirror and then softly so as not to disturb—or alert—Juhanah in the next room, she opened the door and tiptoed down the hall.

The palace was quiet, deserted. Kalila remembered Juhanah's words about it being 'shut up like a box' and thought now that was an apt description. Where was everyone? Aarif had brothers and sisters; were they all searching for treasure? Had she really been left alone for nearly two weeks to await her errant groom?

Kalila sighed, then shrugged. She didn't mind being alone. In fact, considering everything that had happened, she actually preferred it.

Yet right now, in the darkness and the quiet, she felt just a little bit lonely.

She tiptoed gingerly down the main staircase into the front foyer. Even down here everything was quiet and dark. She peeked in a few ornate reception rooms; they all looked formal, unwelcoming. For receiving dignitaries, not for living.

She wandered down another corridor, towards the back of the palace, where the private quarters were more likely to be. It wasn't until she saw the spill of lamplight from a half-open door that she admitted to herself she hadn't just been exploring; she'd been looking for Aarif.

And as she peeked round the door she saw she had found him.

He sat in a comfortable, silk-patterned chair, his spectacles perched on his nose, his head bent over a book.

She took a step into the room, but Aarif was too engrossed in whatever he was reading to notice. What weighty tome was he perusing now? Kalila wondered with a wry smile. The current market prices for diamonds? Some boring business text? It wasn't until she was only a few feet from him that he saw her, and by then she'd read the title of his book, a bubble of laughter rising in her throat and spilling out before she had a chance to suppress it.

'*Agatha Christie?*'

Aarif closed the book, a look of guilty irritation flashing across his face. 'Occasionally I enjoy a respite from the cares of work,' he said stiffly. 'And fiction provides it.'

'Undoubtedly,' Kalila agreed, smiling. The fact that he read light mysteries made him seem more human, more real. Warm. 'I like Agatha Christie too. Tell me, do you prefer Poirot or Miss Marple?'

A smile flickered and died, but even that tiny gesture gave Kalila some hope. Hope of what—? She wouldn't answer that question, but she knew she was glad for whatever link had been forged between them.

'Poirot, of course,' Aarif said. Again the smile, like sunlight breaking through the shadows. He paused. 'And you?'

'Poirot. I always thought Miss Marple a bit stuffy.'

He chuckled, little more than a breath of sound, and then the smiles died on both of their faces as the silence between them stretched into tension, memories. Aarif glanced away.

'Is there something I can help you with, Princess?'

'Are you going to take that tone with me all the time?' Kalila demanded, and Aarif turned back to her with a cool smile, his eyebrows raised.

'I don't know what you mean.'

'That indifferent tone, like you don't know or care about me,' Kalila snapped, goaded into more honesty than she wished to reveal.

Aarif hesitated. 'I think, perhaps,' he said quietly, 'it is better for both of us. Safer.'

Now it was her turn to challenge him with a cool smile of her own. 'I think the time for safety has come and gone.'

Aarif's expression hardened. 'Perhaps, but just because I made one mistake does not mean I wish to repeat it. I think it is wiser for us to maintain our separate existences in the palace, Kalila. At least until my brother returns.'

Kalila pursed her lips. 'And what shall I do for the next two weeks?'

For a moment—a second—Aarif looked discomfited. 'Do…?' he began, and Kalila cut him off with a sharp laugh.

'Other than languish in my bedroom, eating bonbons,' she filled in for him. 'There's no one here, Aarif. I'm alone, and I'm sure there are things I should do before my wedding. You told my father there were preparations, it was why I had to leave so suddenly! Yet now I'm supposed to wander this palace like Bluebeard's bride?'

Aarif's mouth twitched in an involuntary smile even though the rest of his expression remained obdurate. 'It is not my job to entertain you.'

'Isn't it?' she challenged. 'What would your brother say if he knew you were ignoring me? Didn't he instruct you to take care of me?'

'He instructed me,' Aarif bit out, 'to protect you, and I failed. I prefer not to do so again.'

Kalila took a step back at the savagery of his words, his tone. She'd been enjoying their verbal sparring for a moment, had found a freedom in words. She was restless, edgy, unfulfilled, yet release would not come this way.

'Where are you brothers and sisters?' she asked after a moment, and Aarif shrugged.

'Busy.'

'Will they return for the wedding?'

'Undoubtedly.' He did not sound concerned.

Kalila sank into a chair across from him, gazing blankly around the room, a library she realised distantly, taking in the shelves of leather-spined books, the comfortable chairs. It was a room to curl up, to lose yourself, in, amidst many of the stories housed here.

Her gaze found its way back to Aarif, his face still hard, unyielding, and she felt a stab of wounded disbelief that she'd held this man in her arms, had kissed him, touched him. It seemed so incredible now, as if the entire episode were a dream.

Perhaps it was, or as good as.

'I didn't expect it to be like this,' she confessed quietly.

'Nor did I,' Aarif returned, and she thought she heard a current of sorrow in his voice, underneath his carefully neutral tone.

She sighed. 'Aarif, I know—considering what has happened between us—things are difficult, but couldn't you at least extend your hand to me these next weeks? I would like to see this island, the city.' She swallowed, feeling vulnerable and needy and not liking it. 'I want to know the country where I am to be queen, and I can't explore it on my own.'

Aarif was silent, but she saw the reluctance in his eyes, in the tightening of his mouth. She knew the battle warring within him: the desire to serve his brother best, and the duty to stay away from her. And perhaps, with that, a desire to spend time with her? To get to know her, the real her, whoever that was?

She wasn't sure herself; she only knew she'd felt more real and sure and right when she'd been in Aarif's arms.

'Yes, I could do that,' he finally agreed, the reluctance pronounced now, the words drawn slowly out of him. 'I could take you round Serapolis tomorrow if you like.'

Kalila smiled, suddenly feeling light. It was silly to feel so hopeful, as if he'd given her far more than an unwilling tour of the town, yet she did. She had time with Aarif…only hours, and who knew what could happen?

What did she *want* to happen?

The question unsettled her, made her uneasy.

You're thinking you've fallen in love with me. Aarif's warning, an ever present, insistent echo in her heart. She hadn't, she knew she hadn't.

But she could.

Kalila swallowed. 'Thank you,' she whispered, and Aarif jerked his head in the semblance of a nod.

There was no reason to stay in the warm, lamp-lit intimacy of that room, the sound of cicadas a loud chorus through the open windows. Yet she wanted to. She wanted to curl up in a chair and tell Aarif things she'd not told anyone else.

Sometimes I feel like I don't know who I am. I'm caught between two worlds, two lives, and I wonder if I chose the wrong one.

She bit her lip to keep from spilling such secrets, for she knew Aarif did not want to hear them. Worse, he would think less of her if he knew she thought such things. Wouldn't he? Or would he perhaps understand? She'd seen that flicker of compassion before, had felt it like a current between them.

She wanted that feeling again; she didn't want to go. She didn't want to leave him.

'Perhaps I'll get a book,' she said, and stood up, roaming the shelves. 'Any more Agatha Christies here?' she asked, trailing a finger along the well-worn spines.

Aarif sighed. 'I'm afraid not.'

No, she saw, the shelves were filled with dusty old classics, and, like Aarif, she wanted something light. She wanted escape.

'Ah, well,' she said with a little smile and a shrug, and selected a volume at random.

She plopped down into a chair across from him and with a sunny smile opened the book.

It was in German. She stared blankly at the words, fixing a look of interest to her face, although why she was pretending she had no idea.

Aarif sighed, a smile lurking in his eyes even though his mouth was still no more than a hard line. 'Can you read German, Kalila?'

She glanced up, the answering smile in her heart finding its way to her lips. 'No, can you?'

'No, but my father could. Most of these books were his.' His lips twitched. 'How long were you going to stare at that book, pretending you could read it?'

'I'm not sure.' Kalila closed the book with both reluctance and relief. 'I don't want to be alone,' she said quietly, and saw Aarif stiffen.

'It is not appropriate for—'

'Oh, Aarif, hasn't the time for such things passed?' Kalila cut him off. 'What harm can come of us sitting here, in a library?' Yet even as she said the words she heard the answer in her own heart. The room was cast into pools of light and shadow by the little lamp and the thick, velvety darkness outside. It was an intimate environment. A dangerous one, and as Kalila watched Aarif's eyes flare with awareness she knew he realised it too.

She felt it herself, coiling around her heart, making her body tingle. It would be so easy, she thought, to rise from her chair and go to Aarif, to take the spectacles from his nose and the book from his hands, and—

'Go to bed, Kalila,' Aarif said quietly. 'It is late.'

It wasn't that late, only nine o'clock or so, but Kalila knew what he was really saying. *Stay away from me.*

And yet she couldn't. She didn't want to, even though it was dangerous. Even though it was wrong.

Aarif continued gazing at her, his expression steady and becoming cold, the warm, sensual atmosphere dissolving into arctic awkwardness. After a moment Kalila rose from the chair, trying to keep her dignity although it was hard. Aarif said nothing, just watched as she took a step backwards.

'Goodnight,' she finally whispered, and turned around and fled.

It took her a while to find her way back to the bedroom, and Kalila was glad. For a few minutes she lost herself in the darkened corridors, her footsteps a whispery slapping sound against the worn stone. She didn't want to return to her bedroom, her prison.

This is my life now. All of this, my life.

She closed her eyes. How could she have not realised how this would feel? A loveless marriage, born of duty? Hadn't she realised in Cambridge, back when she had had a choice or at least the semblance of one, how this would feel?

How miserable she would be?

And yet, it didn't matter, because in the end, even when she'd found something different, deeper with Aarif—maybe—she would still do her duty, would have to, and so would he. That was what hurt most of all.

She slipped into her bedroom, a cool evening breeze blowing in the scent of jasmine from the gardens.

Kalila went to the window seat and curled up there, her flushed cheek pressed against the cool stone. She gazed down at the shadowy tangle of bushes and shrubs below, and it reminded her so much of her garden at home—a garden she'd loved, a garden she didn't know when she'd see again— that she let out an involuntary choked cry of despair.

I don't want to be here.

A tear trickled down her cheek, and a knock sounded on the door.

Kalila slid from the window seat, dashing that one treacherous tear from her face, and went to open the door. Aarif stood there, his face drawn, as ever, into harsh lines, his eyes dark and almost angry, his mouth pursed tightly.

'Is something wrong…?' Kalila asked and Aarif thrust something at her.

'Here.'

Kalila's hands closed around the object as a matter of instinct and she glanced down at it. It was a book, a mystery by Agatha Christie, one she hadn't read. Her lips curved into an incredulous, hopeful smile and she glanced up at Aarif.

'Thank you.'

'I thought you might want something to read, and I had some in my room.' Then, as if he'd said too much, he shut his mouth, his lips pressed tightly together once more.

Yet Kalila could not keep from smiling, couldn't keep the knowledge from blooming inside her. Somewhere, somehow, deep inside, Aarif cared. About her. Maybe just a little bit, a tiny bit, but—

It was there.

'Thank you,' she said again, her voice dropping to a whisper, and Aarif looked as if he might say something. He raised his hand, and Kalila tensed for his touch, wanting it, needing it—but he dropped it again and gave her a small, sorrowful smile.

'Goodnight, Kalila,' he said, and turned and walked slowly down the darkened hallway.

He needed to stay away from her. Aarif knew that, knew it with every instinct he possessed, and yet he denied what his mind relentlessly told him, denied and failed.

Failed his brother, failed himself, failed Kalila. Was there any test he would not fail? he wondered cynically, his mouth twisting in bitter acknowledgement of his own weakness. Was there anything—anyone—he could be trusted with?

The last time he'd been entrusted with another's care, his brother had died.

Take care of him.

He hadn't.

This time, he'd stolen a princess's innocence, her purity. He had, Aarif acknowledged with stark clarity, ruined her life. For even if Zakari could forgive his bride, the chances of Kalila gaining what she so wanted with him—love, happiness—were slim. How could those be built on a basis of betrayal?

It was with a rare irony that Aarif acknowledged how this tragedy had sprung from the first. If he hadn't had his old nightmare, Kalila wouldn't have comforted him. He wouldn't have found a moment's peace, a moment's sanctuary in her arms, and sought more.

More.

He'd denied himself for so long, kept himself apart from life and love, and yet for a moment he'd given in, he'd allowed himself to feast at a table where he was not even a guest.

And he wanted more.

Even now, he wanted to feel her in his arms, breathe in the sweet scent of her hair, watch the impish smile play about her mouth before he kissed her—

He strode into his bedroom, his fingers threading through his hair, fists clenched, feeling pain—

How could he make this right? How could he make anything right?

Or was he condemned to the hell of living with his mistakes and their endless repercussions, without any chance for healing or salvation?

Outside the cicadas continued their relentless chorus and the moon rose in the inky sky. He was condemned, Aarif decided grimly, and he deserved to be.

CHAPTER SEVEN

THE next day dawned bright and clear, with a refreshingly cool breeze blowing in from the sea. A perfect day for sightseeing, Kalila decided happily as she dressed in loose trousers and a tunic top in a pale mint green.

'What shall we do today?' Juhanah asked, bustling in just as Kalila began plaiting her hair.

Kalila's heart sank. In all her vague imaginings of the day ahead, she had not considered Juhanah, but of course her nurse would expect to accompany her into town, and of course Aarif would demand such a chaperone. Suddenly the day took on a whole new complexion, as Kalila envisioned the many ways Aarif could keep from engaging with her at all.

And wasn't that really the right thing to do? Kalila's conscience suffered yet another pang. If she had any sense of honour or duty, any sense at all, she would keep her distance from Aarif, just as he was determined to keep it from her. Surely learning more about him—growing closer, if such a thing were possible—would only lead to complications. Disappointment. Danger.

And yet. And yet…she still wanted to know him, wanted to discover what drove him, as well as what made him smile or laugh. Wanted to feel that closeness, that connection again. Right now it felt like the only pale ray of hope and happiness in an otherwise dull and disappointing existence.

'Prince Aarif is taking us into Serapolis,' Kalila said, finally answering her nurse. She kept her gaze on her own reflection in the mirror, although she was conscious of Juhanah stilling behind her. 'He realised he has certain duties as host, especially considering there is no one else here at the moment.'

Juhanah gave a small grunt of satisfaction. 'Did you speak to him?'

Kalila hesitated, and in the mirror she saw Juhanah's eyes narrow. 'He gave me a book last night,' she finally said lightly. 'An Agatha Christie, actually. You know how I like mysteries.'

Juhanah still looked suspicious, but she set about folding clothes and rustling the bed sheets, although Kalila was sure there was a palace maid who could see to such things. 'Did he tell you when King Zakari will be returning?'

'No, we didn't speak of it,' Kalila replied, then

bit her lip at that unintentional admission. Juhanah's eyes narrowed speculatively once more.

'Didn't you?' she said, but left it at that.

Aarif met them in the palace courtyard. He looked fresh and cool, dressed in a cream-coloured shirt, open at the throat, and dark, belted trousers.

'We can take a car into the Old Town,' Aarif said, 'which will be comfortable and more private. Or, if you prefer, we can walk. Serapolis is a small city, and we do not have many formal customs here.'

'Let's walk,' Kalila said immediately, and the corner of Aarif's hard mouth twitched upward in a tiny smile.

'I thought you'd say that,' he murmured, and just from his look Kalila felt a dart of electricity shoot straight through her belly, tingling upwards and outwards to every finger, toe, fibre and sinew. She smiled back, but Aarif had already turned away and began to address Juhanah.

That was how the first hour passed as they walked down the narrow, winding street from the palace into the heart of the Old Town. Aarif pointed out various landmarks on the way, but as this was more for the benefit of Juhanah than her, Kalila found her mind drifting.

This was her town, her country. Her life. Her mind skittered away from that thought, although it was difficult to ignore the admiring gazes and bows of passers-by who recognised Aarif, some also guessing who Kalila must be. Within a short while she had collected a handful of ragged posies, and the edge of her tunic was grimy from the hands of children who had come begging for a blessing, some speaking in Arabic, some in Greek, some even in English.

Something softened and warmed inside her at the genuine goodwill of the Calistan people, and she smiled and touched the children's heads, grateful for their spontaneous affection. If she couldn't have the love of her husband, perhaps she would satisfy herself with the love of her people. Many a queen had done the same.

But I want more. The protest rose within her, unbidden, desperate. More.

Out of the corner of her eye she saw Aarif watching her, and there was a strange, arrested look in his eyes, something she didn't understand. She didn't know whether to be alarmed or appreciative of that look, yet it warmed her to know he was looking at her, thinking of her. Conscious of her eyes upon him, he jerked his own gaze away, focusing on the view of the market square ahead of them.

The market was lined with stalls and filled with the raucous shrieks of the peddlers determined or perhaps desperate to sell their wares. Kalila walked along the stalls, revelling in the variety of sights, smells and sounds. It had only been two days ago that she'd been in Makaris, enjoying a sight just like this one, and yet it felt an age, a lifetime ago. Two lifetimes—for surely she was not the same woman she had been then.

She knew she wasn't.

Juhanah was already exclaiming over a bolt of red damask threaded with gold, and Kalila paused before a display of lavender silk, threaded with a rainbow of shades of blue and purple. It looked and felt like water, clean and cool.

'You like that?' Aarif asked, coming up behind her, and Kalila smiled.

'It's very pretty.'

Aarif barked a few instructions in Arabic to the peddler, who, giving him a rather toothless smile, said something back. They were speaking too fast for Kalila to catch what they were saying, and her Arabic wasn't very good anyway, but she knew they were haggling, and she enjoyed seeing the glint of amused determination in Aarif's eyes, the way the simple exchange lightened his countenance.

Finally they reached an agreed price, and Kalila couldn't help but murmur, 'Did you get a good deal?'

Aarif turned to her with a smile and a shrug. 'He would have been offended if I hadn't haggled.'

'Of course.' She paused, watching as the peddler bundled the silk up and Aarif gave instructions to deliver it to the palace. 'You didn't have to buy it for me,' she said quietly.

He shrugged, yet this time the movement lacked the easy familiarity of a moment before. Instead it was tense, straining towards indifference, and his gaze did not meet hers. 'It will look lovely on you. Besides, it is custom in Calista to offer a wedding gift for the bride.'

'Shouldn't that be Zakari's providence?' Kalila asked, then wished she hadn't when Aarif's expression closed up.

'Perhaps, but he is not here to do it,' he replied, and there was a surprising note of acerbity to his voice. For a second Kalila wondered if Aarif was actually criticising his brother.

'Thank you,' she said, and dared to lay a hand on his arm. Aarif stilled, glancing down at her hand, and Kalila was conscious of the warmth of his skin on her fingers, the awareness that surged through her from the simple touch. Would he always affect her this way? she wondered. It was a wonderful and yet frightening thought.

'You're welcome,' Aarif replied, and he raised his gaze so his eyes were steady on hers, like a rebuke. Blushing a little, Kalila removed her hand.

They moved on, past the cloth and fabric stalls with their bolts of silks and satins, as well as the cheaper and more serviceable cotton and corduroy, and onto the spice stalls, with their exotic scents and deep colours of ochre and umber, canisters full of cinnamon, cardamom, paprika and the precious saffron.

There were more stalls, some selling postcards, some cheap American knock-offs and dodgy-looking electronics.

Kalila enjoyed the shouting and shrieking, the bargaining and haggling, the pulsing sense of energy and excitement that a crowded market created. She felt alive, part of something bigger than herself, and it was a blessed escape from the prison of her bedroom and, worse, of her own mind.

Aarif suggested they have lunch at a highbrow-looking restaurant with private rooms and deep, plush chairs, but Kalila refused, wanting to stay out in the noise and tumult of the market. She had a sudden fear that she would lose him in the oppressive formality of such a place; out here, in the market, he was more accessible, more free, and so was she.

They ate greasy, succulent kebabs at a food stall, licking their fingers and washing it down with bottles of warm Orangina, and yet Kalila found it to be one of the best meals she'd ever eaten, with the sun warm on her head, Aarif's eyes warm on her face.

He didn't smile, didn't even unbend, and yet she felt something had changed, shifted imperceptibly between them, and she was glad. It reminded her of how his skin had felt against hers, his lips on hers, and with an inward shiver she knew she wanted to feel that again.

To feel the intimacy of touch, and yet a deeper intimacy too, one of spirit. It amazed her even now that she'd felt that with Aarif…Aarif, who was so hard and dark and harsh. And yet she had; she knew she had, and it felt like something precious, something sacred.

After lunch they wandered around the other side of the market square, where the common hucksters performed their stunts to a half-indifferent, half-enchanted crowd: snake charmers, with the dozy cobras coiled in their baskets, weaving their heads sleepily upwards, the flame-throwers and fire-eaters, and a grinning 'dentist', armed as he was with a basket of pulled, yellowed teeth and a pair of rusty pliers.

'He's just there to scare what tourists come our way,' Aarif murmured in her ear. 'We have a national health service, and I can assure you he is not employed by it.'

Kalila smothered a laugh. 'You mean you haven't used his services yourself?'

Aarif's smile gleamed, white and whole. 'Most assuredly not.'

His hand came around her elbow, guiding her to the edge of the market square. 'Your nurse is flagging,' he remarked quietly. 'I think it might be time to sit down. She looks as if her feet are killing her.'

Guiltily Kalila threw a look behind her, where Juhanah lagged back a few paces. Her nurse did look tired, and her pinched expression suggested that she would indeed prefer a rest.

'Why don't we take tea?' Aarif suggested. 'You might have preferred eating standing up in the street, but I don't think your nurse did.'

'I'm sorry, Juhanah,' Kalila said, coming to take the older woman's arm. 'I've been so enjoying the sights, I haven't thought enough of you.'

'And enjoying more than the sights, it would seem,' Juhanah huffed under her breath, and Kalila shot her a sharp look. Were her feelings for Aarif so obvious? She barely knew what they were herself.

Aarif guided them to a flat-roofed café on the north end of the square. Once inside they were greeted with a flurry of excited chatter interspersed with bows, and then they were taken up a narrow staircase to the roof, open to the sun and sky.

They sat down at a shaded table and a dark-coated waiter soon arrived with glasses of mint tea and a plate of salted pistachios.

They sipped and nibbled in silence for a moment, the sounds of the market below carried on the breeze.

'Thank you,' Kalila said at last, 'for showing me Serapolis.'

'There's much more to see,' Aarif replied with a tiny smile and a shrug. 'Although nothing is quite as exciting as the central square on market day.'

'I'm glad to have seen it.'

Aarif raised his eyebrows. 'You must have seen similar sights back in Zaraq. Makaris's market looked quite like ours.'

'Yes,' Kalila agreed slowly, 'it is, and yet there is something different here.' She looked around at the market below them, and then at the sea, a glinting jewel-green on three horizons. 'There's more of an international flavour here,' she said at last, 'an energy. In Zaraq, we are cut off from most of the world by mountains. It is what has kept us from being invaded, but it has also kept us isolated.'

'Yet your country is very Western and progressive.'

'On the surface,' Kalila agreed after a moment, 'if not in reality.' She pressed her lips together and looked away, but she was still conscious of Aarif's frown.

'What are you speaking of?' he asked after a moment. He rolled the tall glass of mint tea, beaded with moisture, between his palms as he looked at her thoughtfully. 'Are you referring to your marriage?' he continued quietly, although Kalila thought she heard an edge to his voice. 'Arranged as it has been?'

She shrugged. 'Not very Western, that.'

'But necessary.'

'Yes.'

'You could have refused your father,' Aarif said after a moment. 'When you were in Cambridge.' He leaned forward, his expression suddenly intent. 'You could have said no.'

Kalila glanced up from her drink, her eyes widening as she realised what he'd said. What he'd guessed. For that was exactly the temptation that had assailed her in Cambridge, that forbidden, wonderful thought of what could be…but never would.

'Yes,' she said slowly, 'I could have, I suppose. But I knew I never would.'

'Why not?' Aarif demanded, and Kalila shrugged.

'Because. I couldn't betray my family, my heritage,' she stated simply. 'It would be the same as betraying myself.'

Aarif looked away again, yet Kalila had the strange sensation that her answer had somehow satisfied him. She glanced at Juhanah and saw that the older woman had succumbed to the pleasures of a drowsy afternoon in the sun, and was now dozing, her chin nodding against her chest. She turned back to Aarif, a smile glimmering in her eyes, playing around her mouth.

'We wore her out.'

Aarif smiled faintly. 'So it would seem.'

She couldn't resist taking advantage of the privacy afforded by Juhanah's momentary nap. Kalila leaned forward. 'What about you, Aarif? What brought you back to Calista? Were you ever tempted to stay in Oxford, make a life there?'

His fingers flexed around his glass. 'No.'

'Not at all?' Kalila persisted, trying to tease, yet sensing a deeper darkness to Aarif's words, seeing it in his frown.

'No, my duty has always been here. There was never any question of anything else.' He spoke flatly, his eyes on the horizon, or perhaps lost in a memory.

'You always wanted to manage Calista's diamonds?'

He shrugged. 'Always, no. But for many years…' he paused, and Kalila felt as if he was weighing his words, his thoughts. 'Yes,' he finally said, and left it at that.

'What about one of your other brothers?' Kalila asked. 'Are they interested in the diamond industry?' She snagged on a sudden memory. 'Don't you have a twin?'

'Yes, and he has his own affairs to occupy him,' Aarif replied. He drained his glass and set it on the table. 'Now the day is late and it is not good for any of us to sit out too long in the sun. Why don't you wake your nurse and we can go.' He rose from the table to settle the bill, leaving Kalila feeling dismissed. She'd asked too many questions, she knew. She'd tried to get too close.

And yet she'd been closer than this—and closer still—the night in the desert. She couldn't forget that wonderful moment of surprising intimacy, yet, watching the indifferent expanse of Aarif's broad back as he moved through the tables, she felt with a pang of weary sorrow that he could.

Kalila roused Juhanah, who insisted she'd not been asleep at all, but merely resting her eyes, and they made their way back to the palace in rather sombre silence.

A liveried servant swept the front door open and as soon as they were in the foyer Aarif bowed and, with a polite, formal thanks for their company, he took his leave.

Kalila watched him go with a sense of disappointed loss. She had a feeling Aarif would make sure she didn't see him again any time soon. He'd done his duty and taken her out, shown her the city. Now he would find excuses to stay away, and Kalila couldn't think of any to see him again. She envisioned a week of meals in her room, followed by a sudden and inexplicable wedding, and felt the loss intensify inside her.

Back in her bedroom the late afternoon sunlight sent long, lazy shadows across the floor, and the ceiling fan whirred slowly above them, creating barely a stir of air.

There, on her bed, was a paper-wrapped package, and before she'd even touched it Kalila knew what it was.

Her silk. The silk Aarif had chosen for her, had said would look lovely on her—

Kalila choked back a sudden sob, pressing her fist to her mouth. She couldn't cry now, not when it was too late, when nothing could be done—

'Oh, Kalila.' Juhanah stood in the doorway, her fists on her hips. 'What foolish thing have you done, my child?'

Kalila blinked back tears. 'N-n—nothing—'

'You have fallen in love, haven't you?' Juhanah closed the door, shaking her head as she moved closer to Kalila and laid a heavy, consoling hand on her shoulder. 'You miss the king, and so you have taken the prince instead.' Kalila heard both sympathy and censure in Juhanah's voice. 'Haven't you?'

Kalila closed her eyes. She was too tired and heart-sore to deny it, so she said nothing. Juhanah clucked her tongue and sighed.

'It is unfortunate, of course, but it will pass. It is only because the king was not here to see you, and in your disappointment you looked to someone else.'

Kalila kept her eyes closed, her face averted. She wasn't in love with Aarif, she told herself fiercely. He had moments of kindness, of softness, but that was all—

'I'm not in love with him.' There. That had come

out strong, sure. She opened her eyes and blinked back the last sting of tears. 'He has been kind, Juhanah, and I'm homesick and lonely. But it is no more than that.'

'No, indeed.' Juhanah's voice was sharp with suspicion and her fingers tightened on Kalila's shoulder. 'Nothing happened when you ran off?' she asked. 'You were gone a full night—'

'Juhanah!' Kalila made herself sound shocked. She shrugged off her nurse's hand and moved to put the silk away. 'What are you talking about? Prince Aarif found me in the morning. He told you that himself.'

'Yes…' Juhanah let her breath out slowly, and then gave a little nod, seemingly satisfied.

Kalila didn't realise how hard and fast her heart was beating until her nurse left the room. She moved to the window, her hands pressed to her flushed cheeks, and tried to still her racing heart.

If Juhanah discovered what had happened, she trusted her nurse not to say anything, yet she didn't think she could bear her disappointment. And yet what did it matter if Juhanah found out? If anyone found out?

The only person who couldn't find out was Zakari, and Aarif was determined to tell him. And what would happen then? Any chance of happiness—she'd given up on love—would be destroyed. Zakari would hate her, and even if he

forgave her their relationship would always be
tainted with betrayal, *her* betrayal—

She would live under a shadow, a stain that could
never be cleaned away. The thought was crippling,
devastating.

She couldn't let that happen. Not for her sake,
for Zakari's sake, for the sake of the country. Not
for Aarif's sake.

Taking a deep breath, Kalila felt her determination harden into resolve. Tonight she would find
Aarif again, and make him understand.

After another quiet meal in her bedroom with
Juhanah, Kalila dismissed her nurse, insisting that
once again she was tired and wished only to sleep.
Juhanah, however, was less likely to believe this
tale, and left with only the greatest reluctance and
eyes narrowed in suspicion.

Kalila waited a full hour before she slipped from
her room; by that time the dark, quiet corridors
were lit only by moonlight and she could hear
Juhanah's snores through the door of her bedroom.

It took her a while to find her way through the
winding corridors of the palace, and when she did
finally stumble upon the library it was dark and
empty. Disappointment echoed through her as she
surveyed the silent room. She'd been counting on
Aarif being there.

Waiting for her? a sly inner voice mocked, and
Kalila pushed it away resolutely.

She turned away, at a loss. The night stretched emptily, endlessly in front of her.

'Princess?' A disembodied voice floated through the darkness, and Kalila stiffened. The lights flickered on, bringing a mundane yet welcome reality to the situation, and a servant bowed before asking, 'May I help you, Princess?'

'I…' She licked her lips, her cheeks flushing. She felt as if she'd been caught sneaking around after bedtime, and yet in little more than a week she would be mistress of this place. The realisation made her straighten and look at the man with dignity. 'I was looking for the gardens,' she said. 'I would like some fresh air.'

The servant's face was professionally blank as he inclined his head. 'It is dark out, Princess.'

'I think I can manage,' Kalila returned a bit tartly, and, nodding again, the servant led her down another tangle of corridors to a heavy wooden door that clearly led outside.

'I'll wait for you here,' he said, and Kalila replied a bit sharply.

'Thank you, but that's not necessary. I'm quite sure I can find my way back.' In fact she wasn't, but she didn't want a guardian.

Once out in the cool darkness of the garden she wandered down a twisting path lined with palm trees, the cloying scent of jasmine heavy on the air. What to do now? Where to go? She felt as lonely and lost as a little girl, and wished she didn't. Suppressing a sigh that would just tumble her straight into self-pity, Kalila wandered for a few moments until the surprising sound of splashing pulled her curiously in the direction of the noise.

She came round another corner, half expecting to see a pool or fountain, and instead came face to face with Aarif.

He wore only a towel around his hips, his chest bare and brown and beaded with droplets of water. Kalila stared. She'd never seen his chest, only felt it against her own skin, and now she was transfixed by the sight of the lean, hard muscle.

Aarif muttered an oath under his breath when he saw her, and whirled around, jerking the shirt he'd held in his hand over his head. Yet still in that brief moment Kalila saw his back, watched as the moonlight bathed the scars there that she'd felt with her fingertips. They were old scars, long, jagged lines, and instinctively she knew what they were.

Aarif had been whipped.

She opened her mouth to say something, ask— what?—but Aarif had already turned around, and was buttoning up his shirt with stiff fingers. 'What are you doing out here, Princess?' he asked tightly.

'What were you doing?' Kalila challenged. 'Is there a pool out here?'

Aarif raised one eyebrow in surprising,

sardonic amusement. 'There must be, unless I jumped in a fountain.'

Kalila smiled at the mental image. 'Can you show me it?'

'Do you want to go swimming at this hour?'

She shrugged, not willing to admit she just wanted to be with him. 'Why not? You did.'

'You're not wearing a swimming costume.'

She smiled, the gesture innately coy. 'Do I need one?'

Aarif's expression froze, and Kalila wished she hadn't been so provocative. Then he swivelled on his heel and she followed him down the shadowy path.

They came out into an open courtyard, and in the darkness the pool was no more than a glint of moonlight on the water, the sound of the water lapping against the sides. Kalila regarded it for a moment, feeling slightly silly. She was not about to go swimming.

'Do you like to go swimming?' she asked, and her voice sounded false and bright.

'I have made myself like it,' Aarif replied, which was a strange enough answer to make Kalila curious and want to know more.

'Made yourself? You didn't before?'

'I nearly drowned as a young man. It left an impression.'

Kalila could just imagine how resolutely Aarif

would conquer his fears, forcing himself to swim even when it was the last thing he wanted.

'It looks like a lovely pool,' she said lamely, and in the moonlight she could see Aarif's hard expression. All the things she'd been wanting to say—confront him with—died too, withered under that expression.

'Have you heard from Zakari?' she finally asked in a small voice.

Aarif's tiny hesitation told her all she needed to know. 'No,' he admitted, 'but he is likely to be in contact soon.'

'How thoughtful of him,' Kalila snapped.

Aarif shrugged. 'Considering the circumstances, I would've thought you'd be grateful for a reprieve.'

A reprieve. It sounded so grim, so grisly. 'Perhaps,' Kalila allowed, 'but I don't like feeling completely unimportant, either. I feel like I've been discarded—' she took a breath, daring, needing 'twice—'

Aarif stilled. 'There was nothing between us, Kalila,' he said quietly. 'Do not make it so simply because you are unhappy and alone.'

The truth of his words stung, and yet she also knew it was more than that, deeper than that. 'Do you feel anything for me, Aarif?' she asked, grateful for the darkness that hid her burning cheeks. She hated having to be so open, so vulnerable, knowing it would only lead to a rejection painful in its bluntness. Still, she had to ask. She needed to know. 'Did you feel anything for me that night?' she whispered.

Aarif was silent, and in the moonlight Kalila could barely see his face, yet she knew even in the blazing daylight no emotion would be revealed there. He had closed himself off from her already. He was good at that. 'Even if I were in love with you,' Aarif said slowly, heavily, 'it would not matter. Your duty is to my brother, and so is mine.'

'It would matter,' Kalila whispered, her throat aching, 'to me.'

For a moment—a second—she thought he looked torn, perhaps in as much anguish as she was herself. Kalila took advantage of what might be her only opening to reach for him, her hand bunching on the front of his shirt, damp from his skin.

'Aarif, please—' She didn't know what she was asking for, only that she needed him. Needed this, and to her amazement and joy he gave it to her, his hands curling tightly around her shoulders and drawing her to him.

Kalila's head fell back, her lips parting, her eyes closed, waiting—and she felt Aarif hesitate. She knew, even now, that he was struggling, at war with himself, and that the wisest decision, the *right* decision, would be to pull away and leave them both with their dignity and duty.

Yet she didn't. Couldn't, because she wanted

this—him—too much. And when he lowered his head and his lips finally brushed hers, she couldn't keep back the sigh of both pleasure and relief.

How she'd missed this—this closeness, this connection, and of course the pleasure, running through her like honey in her veins, heating her blood, firing her heart. His mouth moved on top of hers, his tongue seeking hers, and then, all too soon, it was over, and he released her with such sudden, savage force that Kalila stumbled backwards.

Still dazed by his kiss, she blinked in the darkness and saw rage flash across his features, spark in his eyes. 'What do you want from me, Kalila?' he demanded, his voice raw. 'You want me to swoon over you, make a fool of myself over you? Do you want my *soul*? Will that help anything? Will it help you when you are married to my brother?' His words were harsh, grating, judging. Desperate. Kalila took a step back.

'No—'

'Here is the truth. I hate myself for what happened between us. I hate myself for betraying my brother, my family, myself, and whatever I could feel for you, if I let myself, is nothing, *nothing* compared to that.' His voice and body both shook, and Kalila could only stare, horrified and humbled by the torrent of emotion pouring through him and into his words.

'Aarif—'

'*That* is how it is between us,' he said flatly, cold and unemotional once more. 'And how it will always be.' He began to stride away, and, desperate not to lose him now, now, when she still felt the taste of him in her mouth, Kalila called after him.

'And what if there is a child?'

Aarif turned around slowly. 'Is that likely, do you think?' he asked in a voice devoid of anything, a voice so cold and distant that it made Kalila cringe.

'I…I don't know,' she admitted, and then, goaded by his cool silence, she added quietly, 'probably not.'

'Then we will, as they say, cross that bridge when we come to it.'

'And you are still determined to tell Zakari?'

'It is hardly something I can keep from him. I am not a liar.'

'I know. I'm not…' Kalila licked her lips. 'Could I tell him instead?'

Aarif stiffened. 'It is my duty—'

'Forget your damned duty!' she cried, her throat hurting from the force of the words, the feeling. 'Nothing is more important to you than that, I *know*, but can you think about what is best for Zakari, for me, for our marriage?' Her voice broke on the word—marriage. 'Instead of using this overblown sense of duty as a salve for your conscience?' she added, knowing she'd said it just to wound, and seeing with savage satisfaction Aarif blink in surprised hurt.

'If you would prefer to tell him,' he said stiffly, 'you may do so.'

Kalila let out the breath she hadn't realised she'd been holding. 'Thank you.'

Aarif nodded, and they were both silent, a silence that ached with sorrow and loss. Kalila wondered why Aarif did not walk away; he simply stood there, staring, as she was, and she wondered what was going through his head, what, apart from his duty, he really wanted.

Did he want her, want more than a stolen kiss in the darkness? Had that night in the desert been a thing apart, born of the storm and the frightful clutch of a nightmare? Had it been no more than a dream?

It had been more. For her, it had been more. Kalila took a breath. 'If you were able to tell me the truth,' she said, 'then I will tell you the truth also. That night in the desert—when I held you in my arms—that was not simply because I was lonely and afraid. It was more than that to me, Aarif. It was real. I didn't love you, because I didn't know you enough, but when you touched me I felt like I *could* love you, and I've never felt that before.' Aarif was silent, and from behind a haze of tears Kalila saw a muscle jerk in his jaw.

She took a step towards him, and then another, until she was close enough to touch him, which she did. She ran one fingertip along the livid line of his scar, traced it as she had that night before cupping his cheek. 'I don't know what haunts you, Aarif,' she whispered. 'What drives you to this sense of duty and despair. Is it guilt? Shame?' She shook her head slowly. 'I wish I could take it from you. I wish I could bear it for you.' His face was still and unyielding under her fingers yet she saw with a little shock that his eyes were closed, as if in pain or anguish, and she felt the connection between them like a current, conducted by her hand on his cheek. 'I wish you would let me,' she added quietly. 'But instead I fear I've only added to it, and of all the reasons to regret what happened between us, that is the greatest of all.'

Underneath her hand she felt Aarif shake his head, and then for the briefest of moments his fingers touched hers, pressed her hand against his cheek before he released her, stepping back.

Kalila swallowed past the lump of misery crowding her throat. 'Goodnight,' she whispered, and then turned and stumbled down the path back to safety. Solitude.

Loneliness.

CHAPTER EIGHT

KALILA awoke from a dreamless yet discontented sleep as Juhanah bustled in with her breakfast tray. After thanking her nurse, she stared dispiritedly at the coffee and *labneh*, her appetite utterly vanished.

Pushing her breakfast away, Kalila clambered out of bed and went to the window. The sun was rising above the sea, sending long golden rays across the gardens. Kalila took a deep breath of the still-cool, dry air and turned to Juhanah.

'I'm not going to stay in the palace today. I'll go crazy if I wait in here all week. I want to go out.'

'We went out yesterday,' Juhanah objected mildly. 'There are the gardens and the pool, Kalila. You could pass the day quite pleasantly.'

An image of Aarif, wet and bare from his swim, rippled across Kalila's mind and she pushed it away. For riding on the heels of that image was another, that of his voice, flat and terrible, as he spoke to her.

Whatever I could feel for you, if I let myself, is nothing, nothing *compared to that.*

Kalila swallowed and shook her head. 'No, I need to do something. Go somewhere—' Her gaze fell on a cluster of buildings in the distance, part of the palace compound, and she smiled. Stables. 'I'm going to ride,' she said resolutely. 'I want to ride.'

'Is that wise, Princess,' Juhanah murmured, 'considering—?'

'I'm not running away,' Kalila cut her off. 'It's too late for that. Anyway, Juhanah, this is an island.' She managed to smile wryly. 'There's nowhere really I can go.'

'We could ask Prince Aarif, I suppose…'

'No.' She didn't want another confrontation with Aarif, not when his judgment was still ringing in her ears. 'We don't need to bother the prince with such a matter,' she said, not quite looking at her nurse. 'He is not my jailor.'

'He is concerned for your welfare—'

'I've been on a horse since I was five. I think I can take care of myself.' Kalila knew she sounded petulant, but she couldn't bear the thought of going to Aarif to seek his permission, seeing him hesitate, perhaps even refuse her request. 'I'm sure there is someone at the palace besides Aarif who can arrange a mount for me,' she said. She'd made arrangements for her own mare, As Sabr, to be transported to Calista, but she knew she would not arrive for some days or weeks.

'I'll see what can be done,' Juhanah said quietly and left the room.

It took over an hour to finally track down a servant who had access to the stables, and then to find and saddle a suitable mount. Kalila was afraid Aarif would round a corner, coldly furious that she would even think of riding out considering what she'd done the last time she'd been on a horse. But he did not appear, and with the sun shining in a dazzling, hard blue sky, she left the palace compound for the flat, open stretch of the desert, undulating endlessly to the horizon.

It felt good to be out beneath the sun and sky, the wind stinging her cheeks, the air fresh in her lungs as she drew breath after deep, cleansing breath. It felt good to be free.

Aarif stared mindlessly at the contract he held in his hand before he shoved it away with an impatient sigh. He had not been able to work this morning; he felt hardly able to think. He was restless and anxious and a little bit angry, and he knew the reason why.

Kalila. He couldn't get her out of his mind. He'd enjoyed their day in Serapolis too much, had felt something lightening and loosening inside him, something that had been held so tightly he'd forgotten how it felt to be free. To smile, to enjoy life.

His mind drifted to last night, that stolen kiss—

it had been so tempting, so sweet, and if he'd let himself he would have made it into more. He'd wanted to drag her down to the wet tiles by the pool and have her right there, bury himself inside her warmth and *forget*…forget for a few moments everything that had made him who he was.

Yet even more wrenching than the memory of the kiss was that of the open, vulnerable honesty in her eyes, the tremulous smile on her face, the tear glistening on her cheek in the moonlight. The way her fingers, cool and smooth, had felt on his face, caressing his scar.

His scar. As a matter of habit and instinct, Aarif's own hand went up to his cheek to trace that grim reminder of his failure. He had never told Kalila about that day, there was no way she could know, and yet somehow she did.

I wish I could bear it for you. It was a testimony to her kindness, her generosity of spirit, that she would wish such a thing. If only she could! Aarif smiled grimly. No one could bear his burden, because it was his guilt, his shame, just as she'd said. And no matter how many times he tried to throw it off, it always came back to settle heavily on his soul.

Aarif…help me…

It was a cry that had been seared into his mind, his heart. A cry he would—could—never forget, and that desperate plea haunted him every day of his life.

Aarif…save me…

And he hadn't.

Aarif pushed away from his desk and stalked out of his office, still restless. He passed a palace servant and barked, 'Do you know where the Princess Kalila is?' He didn't even know why he was asking; he wasn't going to see her, he wasn't—

The servant stiffened and turned. 'She has gone riding, Your Highness.'

'Riding?' Aarif repeated, the word one of disbelief and then dawning fury. 'She has gone riding and no one thought to tell me?'

Fear flickered faintly across the man's features. 'I thought—it was acceptable—'

Aarif jerked his head in a nod, realising how controlling he must sound. Of course it was acceptable. Kalila could do what she liked. She was a princess, soon to be a queen. No one here knew about her attempted escape, and Aarif doubted she would try such a thing again. Where could she go?

And yet his gut churned with anxiety at the thought of her out there alone. Stupid, when she was a capable horsewoman, a grown woman who could—must—make her own decisions. Her own choices. Still, he could not keep back the fear. Always, the fear.

He turned back to the servant who waited uneasily. 'Make arrangements to saddle my horse,' he said brusquely, and strode down the corridor.

* * *

The sun was hot on her bare head, the wind sending her hair streaming behind her in a dark curtain. Kalila urged her mount on, faster, needing the speed, the blur of motion and activity like a drug.

For a moment, she wanted to forget the cares that threatened to topple over, drag her under; for a moment she wanted to be like a child and race the wind.

A fallen palm tree, bleached to bone-whiteness, lay in her path, and, digging her heels into the horse's flanks, she urged the mare onwards. It was a simple, easy jump, and the horse cleared it without trouble. Then a little sand cat scuttled out from under the fallen palm, and the horse reared in surprise.

Kalila could have kept her seat—she almost thought she had—but she'd already cleared the log and had let herself relax. In that unguarded moment she felt herself sliding off, saw the ground rushing to meet her, yet everything seemed to be happening so slowly—then she felt the sharp, sudden pain of her head hitting a rock.

She lay there, dazed and breathless for a moment, thinking she was all right, blinking up at the blue sky. Then, like a dark curtain being drawn slowly across her mind, unconsciousness overtook her.

Later, in the hazy dream-state between sleep and wakefulness, she was aware of someone bending over her, gentle fingers smoothing her hair away from her forehead, a voice, low and sure, murmuring soothingly. She felt herself being lifted into capable arms, and then she slid mercifully back into darkness again.

Some point later, she was in a car, lying down on the back seat, and she felt the cool leather against her cheek. Then darkness again, yet before it drew her in once more she was conscious of one thought—one comfort—Aarif.

He was there. He had found her, and he had taken care of her.

'You're good at that, aren't you?' she half-mumbled, and heard him distantly ask her what she said. 'You take care of people,' she said, the words sounding slurred to her own ears. 'You take care of me.' Her eyes flickered open, and she saw Aarif's face bent over her, his jaw working, a strange sheen in his eyes, but then she was lost again to the comforting darkness of sleep.

When she awoke, sunlight was streaming in a small, bare room from a window high on the wall and she lay in a bed, an unfamiliar bed with crisply starched sheets. A hospital bed.

Kalila tried to move her head, and winced at the pain that sliced through her skull. She tried again, and her gaze rested on the man sitting in a chair by her bed, his head braced against one hand, his thick, luxuriant lashes fanning his cheeks. Aarif, his features softened into sleep, the stubble glinting on his jaw. Kalila wanted to reach out and touch him, but she couldn't summon the energy so she satisfied herself instead with letting her gaze rove hungrily, unfettered, over his profile, the crisp dark hair, the harshly arched eyebrows, the aquiline nose.

Then his eyes fluttered open and captured her gaze with his own, so she was trapped, exposed in her shameless scrutiny of him. A sleepy smile curved Aarif's mouth, and the gaze that stretched between them seemed to wrap Kalila in something warm and safe, like a cocoon.

Then awareness came with wakefulness, and Aarif sat up, running a hand through his hair. 'You're awake.'

Kalila smiled faintly. 'So it would seem. What happened?' Her voice sounded rusty, and she realised her mouth was as dry as dust.

'Would you like some water?'

She nodded gratefully and Aarif poured a glass of water from the pitcher by her table, then held the straw to her lips, the simple gesture somehow tender and intimate. She drank thirstily for a moment before she leaned back against the pillow once more.

'How did you find me?'

'I rode out after you,' Aarif replied, replacing the glass on the table, his face averted.

'Did you think I was running away?' Kalila asked, and though she'd meant the question to be a teasing one she heard the note of hurt that crept into her voice. Aarif heard it too, and he turned to her with a faint, wry smile.

'No. But you are under my care, and I wanted to make sure no harm came to you.'

Kalila nodded. She could hardly chafe at that, when in fact he might have very well saved her life. Who knows what might have happened if she'd been out in the desert heat, alone, unconscious?

'Thank you,' she said. 'For once, I am glad of your sense of duty.'

Aarif's smile deepened briefly before it died. 'For once, so am I,' he agreed.

Kalila lifted one hand to feel the bandage on her head, a thick pad of gauze that seemed to cover half her skull. 'Am I badly hurt?' she asked, and Aarif shook his head.

'A concussion, and they wish to keep you here overnight for observation. But it is no more than that, and there should be, if any, a very little scar.'

She didn't care how big a scar there was, and yet she wondered if Aarif thought she did. His face had reverted to its more usual, expressionless mask, and the sight saddened her.

For a moment, he'd seemed close. For a moment, it had seemed as if he felt for her what she felt—

But what did she feel? What could she feel for

this man who was to be her husband's brother? Fatigue and an overwhelming sense of hopelessness crashed over her in a wave, and Kalila turned her head away.

'Thank you,' she said again, stiffly. 'You can go now. I am sure there is much you have to do, and I don't need a nursemaid.'

She waited, half expecting Aarif to leave with a murmured farewell. Wanting him to leave, because it hurt to have him here, hurt to be near him when she couldn't be with him as she wished, as she needed—

'I don't want to go,' Aarif said in a low voice, and Kalila turned her head back to face him, wincing at the pain the sudden movement caused.

Aarif's expression was one of both anguish and honesty, and it tore at her soul. He was admitting something both wonderful and terrible, and he knew it.

Smiling a little, the expression somehow sad, he reached forward and brushed a tendril of hair away from her face, his fingers trailing gently along her cheek. 'I don't want to go,' he said again, his voice no more than a whisper.

Silently she reached her hand out to clasp his, still on her cheek, pressing his fingers against her face as he had done to her only the night before.

He returned the clasp, his fingers tightening on hers, and they remained like that, silent and touching, for a long time, as the shadows lengthened in the room and the day turned to dusk.

She left the next day. Aarif had spent the night next to her in his chair, although they had not spoken beyond the trivialities. Yet something had shifted, Kalila knew. Something had loosened, and she wondered if it was a good or a bad thing.

It felt good, she knew that. It felt wonderful. Aarif did not speak or even act in a way so different from how he had before, yet it *felt* different. He had acknowledged to himself what he felt for her—or so Kalila hoped—and it broke down the barricade he had erected as a defence between them.

Yet still, she reminded herself bleakly, it changed nothing. Still, in a week she would marry Zakari. She pushed the thought away, desperate to cling to the hope that somehow something could change, that even at the eleventh hour rescue would come.

Her knight in shining armour, she thought wryly, and knew the only knight—the only man—she wanted was Aarif.

He drove her back to the palace that morning and she spent the days mostly resting, regaining her strength for the celebrations and events that lay ahead.

There had still been no word from Zakari, and in a moment of bitterness Kalila remarked to

Juhanah that he was like a phantom prince, never to arrive.

'A king,' Juhanah corrected her with surprising grimness, 'and when he arrives, *ya daanaya*, you will know it.'

Three days after her accident Kalila ventured out to the pool. It was set amidst the luxuriant gardens, surrounded by tumbled rocks and a cascading waterfall so Kalila felt as if she'd stumbled on a bit of Eden, rather than a man-made enterprise. She stretched out on a chaise, fully intending to read the Agatha Christie Aarif had lent her, but it lay forgotten in her hand as she warmed her self and soul under the dry desert sun, lulled to a doze by the tinkling of the waterfall and the swaying of the palms above her.

'You look much better.'

Kalila's eyes flew open. She didn't know how long she'd been lying there, half-asleep, but now she was most certainly wide awake, and aware of Aarif standing above her. He was dressed in crisp trousers and a polo shirt, and he looked clean and fresh. Even though her swimming costume was modest by Western standards, Kalila felt exposed under his bland gaze.

'I feel better,' she allowed.

Aarif was silent for a moment, his expression guarded, and then when he spoke his voice was abrupt. 'I wondered if you'd like to leave the palace compound for a bit. I could show you where the diamonds are mined, as well as a few other of Calista's sights.'

Kalila's heart leapt at the thought. Away from the palace—with Aarif. It was tempting; it was dangerous. 'Yes, that would be nice,' she replied, her voice amazingly level and calm.

'Good.' Aarif nodded. 'We can go after lunch if you like.' Kalila nodded her agreement, and without another word he turned and left.

Her nerves were too highly strung even to consider lounging by the pool with a paperback, so Kalila returned to her room to shower and dress.

A few hours later she had eaten in her bedroom, as usual, and was waiting in the foyer of the palace, dressed in a sleeveless cotton blouse in pale lavender and loose trousers.

She heard footsteps and turned to see Aarif, keys in hand, coming down the stairs. He didn't smile when he saw her, just nodded. 'Good. You're ready.'

He led her outside, and Kalila saw that an open-top Jeep had been driven round. Aarif opened the passenger door for her, and a few minutes later they were speeding away from the palace, away from the narrow, crowded streets of Serapolis, to the open stretch of desert.

They drove in silence, companionable enough, Kalila decided. She was content to simply enjoy the warm, dry breeze on her face, and the sight of the desert stretching away in graceful waves to a jewel-green sea.

'We'll drive to the river first,' Aarif said after a few moments. 'That's where the diamond workshops are.'

Kalila nodded, pushing a strand of hair away from her eyes and wishing she'd brought a hat, or at least a hair clip.

Aarif saw the movement and gave her a sideways smile. 'I'm used to seeing you a bit of a mess,' he said, his voice low. 'I suppose I like it.'

It wasn't really a compliment, yet it still sent delight fizzing through her veins, filling up her head and heart with impossible hopes.

They didn't speak again until the river, a winding stretch of muddy green, came into view, along with a few low, long sheds where Kalila assumed the diamonds were polished and honed.

Aarif parked the Jeep, and as they got out she saw where the diamonds were mined, a side of the rocky bank that was covered with a system of scaffolding and drainpipes.

'The diamonds are difficult to access,' Aarif told her, his hand under her elbow as he guided her along the uneven ground. 'And at present they are mined only by skilled artisans. There is too much corruption in the world of diamond mining as it is.' There was a hard note to his voice.

Kalila nodded, and Aarif led her past the river

to the sheds. Aarif explained the process to her, how the diamonds had to be separated from the silt and gravel, then carefully polished and cut. He unlocked a case to show her a diamond in the rough—it looked no more than a piece of dirty glass, yet once honed it would, Aarif assured her, be quite spectacular.

'I prefer them like this, sometimes,' he said with a small, wry smile. 'Nothing gaudy or showy. All the potential—the best—still to come. The hope.'

Kalila nodded, her throat suddenly tight, for she understood what he meant. There was so much more excitement and hope in possibility, rather than in the finished product, known, certain, dull. She handed him back the diamond. 'Yes, I see what you mean.'

'I'm boring you,' Aarif said as he locked the case up again, and Kalila shook her head. 'I forget sometimes that most people are not interested in this as I am.'

'No, you're not,' Kalila said. 'I like learning about the diamonds—about you.' Aarif kept his face averted, and Kalila took a breath and continued. 'What made you first interested in diamonds?'

Aarif shrugged. 'Someone needed to do it.'

'But you clearly have a passion for it,' Kalila persisted. It had been obvious from his voice, the bright gleam in his eyes.

His hands stilled for a moment on the case, then he tucked the key back in his pocket and shrugged. 'It is important to me,' he said, his voice strangely cautious.

'What did you study at Oxford?' Kalila asked, genuinely curious.

He frowned, then replied, 'Geology.'

It made sense if he were to go into the diamond trade, Kalila supposed, yet with the conversation she felt as if she'd touched something hidden, forbidden. Something Aarif didn't want to talk about.

'What about you?' he asked. 'What did you study at Cambridge? History, your father said, I think?'

Kalila nodded. 'Yes, and then I started my MPhil in medieval social history.' She smiled wryly. 'Not very useful, but I enjoyed it, learning about people and the way they used to live.'

'You started?' Aarif repeated with a frown, and Kalila shrugged.

'I would have finished around now, but—'

'The wedding was delayed so many times,' he murmured. 'I suppose your father wanted you home.'

'Yes.'

His gaze was distant, his hands still in his pockets. 'And so you went.'

'You're not the only one with a sense of duty,' Kalila said, trying to be rueful but sounding a bit sharp. Aarif sent her one swift, searching glance.

'No,' he agreed quietly, 'I'm not.' He moved towards the door. 'There is a restaurant on the beach with a superlative view of the ocean. We can rest there.'

They drove in silence down the long, winding coast road, the sun starting its descent towards the sea, turning its surface to shimmering gold.

The restaurant was perched on a cliff top, with just a few rickety chairs and tables on a terrace, and the lone waiter, agog at serving royalty, nearly tripped over himself to provide them with glasses of orange sharbat and a plate of sticky sesame-coated buns, plump with raisins and sweetened with honey.

They ate and drank, chatting with comfortable ease that soon drifted into companionable silence. After a while, that silence became strained with unspoken tensions, memories, and thoughts. Strange, Kalila thought, how without a word spoken or a look given silence could become charged, dangerous, a palpable energy swirling around them.

Aarif's eyes were on the distant, shimmering sea, his gaze hooded and thoughtful. At that moment he hardly seemed aware of her existence.

Kalila lay a hand on his sleeve, yet he seemed unaware of her touch. 'Aarif, what are you thinking?'

He turned to her slowly, his expression still distant, as if he had yet to wake from the snarl of a dream, or perhaps a memory. 'I was thinking about the sea,' he said after a moment. 'It is so peaceful now, a thing of beauty. And yet it can be so treacherous.'

Despite the warmth of the sun on her shoulders, the gentle maritime breeze teasing her hair away from her face, Kalila wanted to shiver. She did not know what held Aarif in its terrible thrall, yet she sensed it had come to grips with him again.

'The hour is late,' Aarif said abruptly, draining his glass. 'We should return to the palace before people wonder where we are.'

Kalila followed him from the café, the waiter bowing and murmuring thanks behind them. Back in the Jeep, they drove back along the coast road in silence, and as the daylight faded into dusk so, Kalila thought, did that easy, companionable silence she hadn't even realised she'd been cherishing.

She suppressed a sigh, and then turned in surprise when just a mile or two from the palace Aarif pulled off the road onto a lonely stretch of beach.

'What…?'

'I want to show you something,' he said, his voice strangely brusque, and Kalila followed him across the rocky, uneven ground. The sun had faded, leaving only livid purple streaks across the sky and long shadows on the sand.

Aarif walked to within a few feet of the sea, which lapped against the sand with a soft, shushing sound. He gazed out at the sea, his hands thrust deep in his pockets, while Kalila waited behind him, conscious of the now-cool breeze that ruffled her hair and set goosebumps rising along her bare arms.

'I haven't come to this little beach in a while,' Aarif said after a long moment. He turned around, and in the shadowy darkness Kalila saw that he was smiling, although it didn't feel like a smile, and she didn't relax.

Aarif came and sat down on the sand, his elbows resting on his knees. Kalila sat next to him. The sand was cold and hard, and she waited, the only sound the continual lapping of the waves against the shore.

'Sometimes,' Aarif said quietly, 'I feel that my whole life has been bound up in a single moment. Here.' He raised one hand to gesture to the darkening beach before letting it fall once again. 'Everything has been held hostage to what happened here.' He shook his head, and Kalila waited, apprehension seeping through her with the chilling sand. 'When I was fifteen,' Aarif finally continued, 'my brother Kaliq and I decided we wanted a little adventure. We were bored, I suppose, and restless.' He paused, and Kalila wondered if he meant to go on. She could barely see him now, even though he was next to her. Darkness was falling fast. 'We built a raft,' Aarif continued finally. 'Out of driftwood and some rope. It wasn't a particularly handsome craft, but it did the job.' He shook his head, lost once more in memories, and Kalila was left groping in a darkness that had nothing to do with the setting sun. Why was Aarif telling her this now? Was this—an innocent, boyish adventure—the dark memory that snared his dreams and even his desires? She couldn't understand, and she wanted to.

'I don't know what might have happened,' Aarif said slowly, 'if Zafir hadn't found us out. He was my little brother, six years old, and he insisted that he come along with us.' Kalila heard the *was*, and felt another, deeper chill of apprehension. 'I said he could. You see, I was in charge. I always had been. Kaliq and I might be twins, but I was born first and those eight minutes have made all the difference. I've never forgotten that it was my responsibility to look after the younger ones, and especially little Zafir, the apple of my father's eye. There wasn't a soul alive who couldn't love him.' Aarif's voice took on a ragged edge and he turned his head away from Kalila, tension radiating from every taut line of his body.

She raised her hand, wanting to touch him, to take away some of his pain she felt like a physical thing, but he flinched, and she dropped her hand again.

'That raft took us out to sea,' he continued, his voice toneless now. 'We had no idea what we were doing, and before we could even credit it we were over a mile from shore. Then we saw a ship in the distance, and we thought it was our salvation. We flagged it down—took off our shirts and waved them. The ship came closer, and even then we didn't realise…'

'Realise what?' Kalila whispered.

'Diamond smugglers,' Aarif said. 'Modern-day pirates. Perhaps they would have left us alone but Zafir—little Zafir—told them we were the sons of the King of Calista and they would be rewarded for rescuing us.' He smiled bitterly. 'Well, they exchanged reward for ransom, and took us aboard.'

'Oh, Aarif—'

'They took us to a deserted island, one of the many scattered around here, and tied us up like animals. I'd never seen Zafir looking so…so *bewildered*. He'd only encountered goodness in his life, love and warmth, and now this…! At six years old. Those men were fiends. Demons.'

Kalila shook her head, unable to even imagine the terror and helplessness they all must have felt.

'After a few days,' Aarif resumed, 'Zafir loosened his ropes. He managed to untie us both— he was so brave! When our captors were busy— drunk, most like—we tried to escape.' Even in the dusky half-light Kalila could see the bleakness in his eyes, and she felt it in her own soul.

'And?' she whispered, for she knew the story did not end there.

'And we almost made it,' Aarif said. 'We made it back to the raft—they'd left it on the shore, most likely to use for firewood. Then…' he took a breath and let it out slowly. 'They saw us leaving, and they knew if we escaped, they were all dead men. My father would see to it. They had nothing to lose, and so they began shooting. One bullet hit me—little more than a graze, but I fell into the water.' His hand went to touch the scar on his face, although Kalila doubted he was aware of the action. 'I couldn't see for the blood, but I could hear. I heard Kaliq fall in the water too, and Zafir…Zafir…' He broke off with an almost-shudder. A full minute passed and a cold breeze blew off the water. When Aarif spoke again, it was in that terrible, toneless voice that made Kalila want to both weep and shiver. 'The smugglers dragged both Kaliq and me back to shore. But Zafir was lost on the raft. The last thing I saw was him on the horizon, nothing more than a speck. And I *heard* him…' His voice choked before he continued. 'I always hear him, asking me to help him. Save him. Me. He looked to me…and I failed him. I did nothing.' He shook his head, lost in the terrible tangle of his own thoughts.

'What happened then?' Kalila asked eventually, for, although all she wanted to do was put her arms around Aarif and smooth the furrows from his forehead, kiss and comfort his pain and sorrow away, she knew the tale had not ended.

'The smugglers took us prisoner. They were furious—and desperate. They took that out on us, but nothing, *nothing* seemed to matter any more.' Kalila remembered the scars on his back, and knew just what Aarif meant. 'My father paid the ransom, and we were returned. The smugglers were brought to justice, though they sought to escape it. But—' he drew in a breath '—we never saw Zafir again. Not even a trace.'

Kalila swallowed, her eyes stinging. 'I'm so sorry, Aarif.'

'I don't speak of it,' he told her. He turned his head so he was facing her, his eyes dark and determined. Kalila felt a quiver of apprehension ripple through her. 'None of us wish to remember. My father—and even my stepmother—were never the same again after we lost Zafir. It was as if all of our lives had lost an easy joy, and we were never to know it again.'

'It must have been—'

'I'm telling you now,' Aarif cut her off, 'because I want you to understand. When I told my father I would look after Zafir that day, I took it as an oath. A sacred duty, and I failed in the most horrific, spectacular way that I could.'

'But it wasn't your—'

Aarif held up a hand, and the sharp movement silenced her as if he'd put that hand over her mouth. 'I failed, and I shall never forget that I failed. It is a burden I carry to this day, and I shall carry it until I die. But I have alleviated its weight and pain by striving to never fail so again. I devoted my life to my family and this island, and the business of diamonds so that men such as the ones who kidnapped us might not profit and sail freely as they did that day. I honour Zakari as my brother and my king, and now that my father is dead my duty is—always—to him.' He paused, and Kalila knew this was what she did not want to hear. 'No matter what sacrifices I must make, or what pain it causes me.'

Her throat was tight, too tight, so it hurt to swallow. 'Are you talking about me?' she asked finally, her voice no more than a strangled whisper.

'Yes.' Aarif spoke heavily. 'Kalila, I will not lie. When you held me in your arms, I wanted you. I needed you.' His mouth twisted, and Kalila blinked back a haze of tears. 'I've never felt…so…*right* as I did then.' He shook his head. 'Perhaps in time I could have loved you. I have not known many women…I have not allowed myself to. But you…you were different.'

Kalila felt the cold trickle of tears on her cheeks. She held out one hand in supplication, but it was ignored. 'Aarif—'

'No. I tell you this now to spare you pain. I realise in these last few days you have thought yourself in love with me, although I can hardly believe you would love a man such as me—' He stopped, swallowed, and then shook his head when Kalila made to speak. 'And I have reacted with small kindnesses because I still wanted to be near you, to—' he swallowed again, his voice low '—even just to see you smile, to see the light in your eyes. But such things were unfair to you, because they gave you hope. There is no hope, Kalila, for us. There *is* no us. There never can be.'

Kalila's mouth was dry, her heart pounding even as it seemed to break. She forced herself to speak, her voice low and aching. 'Because I am engaged to your brother?'

Aarif nodded. 'Yes, of course.'

'And if I wasn't…?' Kalila asked.

Aarif's brows pulled together in a dark frown. 'There is no point even considering such a thing.'

Kalila knew she shouldn't say it—say anything—but she felt desperate and reckless and so very sad. 'What if I broke the engagement? What if I refused to marry him?'

Aarif's breath came out in a surprised rush, yet he did not speak. The night had fallen completely now, and the sky was inky and scattered with stars. 'If you did such a thing,' Aarif said slowly, 'then you would not be the woman I love.'

The woman I love. Was he saying he did love

her? How could such a wonderful thing cause her such emotional agony? Kalila closed her eyes briefly, and she felt Aarif's fingers caress her face. She leaned into his hand, craving his touch, needing the comfort.

'Come now, *ayni*.' The Arabic endearment slipped off his tongue and made Kalila feel somehow all the more bereft. 'The hour grows dark and we must return to the palace.'

And with that return, Kalila knew she would lose Aarif for ever. Yet how could she lose something she'd never really had in the first place?

Except now, with the lingering memory of his fingers caressing her face, his words *the woman I love* echoing through her heart, she felt as if she'd lost something very precious indeed.

Wordlessly she allowed him to help her up from the hard sand, and they walked in silence to the Jeep.

The lights of Serapolis glittered on the horizon, and in only a few minutes they had driven to the front of the palace. A servant leapt to open their doors, and Aarif handed him the keys. Silhouetted by the light spilling from the open palace doors, he turned to Kalila with a sorrowful smile.

'Goodnight, Princess.'

Kalila's throat was too clogged with tears to respond, and in desperate silence she watched him walk away.

CHAPTER NINE

THE days slid by in a miserable, endless blur. Kalila was conscious of things changing as the wedding day drew nearer. People arrived, guests, more servants, Aarif's brothers and sisters, although not Zakari. He, at least, still saw fit to stay away, and Kalila could only be glad.

Her heart was too full—too broken—to even consider her future, or the wedding that loomed closer every hour. And yet she could not stop the marriage from taking place, the future slowly and surely becoming the present.

The long, empty days in the palace were gone, replaced with a sudden, frenetic activity as everyone in Calista began to prepare and anticipate one of the biggest events of the decade. Her marriage.

There was a flurry of dinners, parties, lunches and teas. The parade of faces were no more than a nameless blur, although Kalila tried to commit them to memory, to greet and chat with Aarif's siblings, although it felt like a parody, no more than play-acting.

Aarif stayed distant, never approaching or addressing her. It was, Kalila thought numbly, as if the past were nothing more than a dream…a wonderful yet terrible dream, for she knew it would torment her every hour of her life.

Two days before the wedding her father, King Bahir, arrived at the palace by helicopter. Along with half a dozen palace servants and Aarif and Kalila met him at the helipad in the palace courtyard. She sneaked a glance at Aarif, but he was turned away from her, standing to attention as the helicopter made its descent.

Her father emerged from the helicopter, and the sight of his familiar face with its kind, dark eyes and ruddy cheeks, the sparse white hair blowing in the wind, made sudden tears sting her eyes and she started forward.

'Papa!' The endearment from childhood sprang naturally to her lips. 'I'm so glad to see you.'

Bahir embraced her before holding her away from him, his eyes narrowing as he took in her appearance. 'And I am glad to see you, daughter.' But Kalila saw the displeasure flash in his eyes, his lips tightening, and she wondered what had made him angry. Had he heard of her desert escapade…or worse?

Aarif cleared his throat before sketching a bow. 'King Bahir, we are honoured.'

'Indeed.' Bahir's gaze was still narrow. 'I may assume by your presence that King Zakari is still away on business?'

'Unfortunately, yes.' Aarif's voice was toneless, and his expression did not flicker for a moment.

'I see.' Bahir nodded, his eyes ever shrewd. 'Then I will take tea in my room, if it can be arranged, Prince Aarif. It was an unsettling flight and I detest flying in helicopters.'

Aarif nodded briskly. 'It shall be done.'

'And the princess,' Bahir continued, 'shall take tea with me. I'm sure we have much to say to one another.'

Upstairs in her father's suite of rooms, Kalila stood nervously by the door while a servant wheeled in a tea trolley. Her father sat at a table by the window, the late afternoon sun creating a golden halo around his head, one leg crossed elegantly over the other.

He waited for the servant to depart before he gestured for Kalila to pour them both tea. She moved forward, her hands shaking just a little bit as she poured the tea out. Bahir watched her silently, and Kalila kept her gaze averted from his all too knowing one.

'You are well?' she finally asked, handing him his glass. Bahir accepted it and took a sip, his eyebrows arched over the rim.

'Yes, I am,' he said after a moment. 'But I would rather hear if you are well.'

Kalila's startled gaze flew to his. 'Y-y-y-yes,' she said, wishing she hadn't stuttered like a guilty child. 'I am.'

Bahir set his glass down carefully. 'Because, Kalila,' he continued gently, 'you don't look well.'

Kalila's gaze moved inadvertently to the mirror hanging above the bureau and she was surprised by her reflection. She hadn't looked at herself properly in days; she'd been moving through the hours like a ghost or sleepwalker, simply tracking time. Now she saw how wide and staring her eyes were, her face pinched and pale. She looked back at her father and saw him looking at her with far too much perception. Perception, she realised, and compassion.

Whatever her father might have heard about her escape to the desert—and Aarif's finding her—he was not angry. He was worried.

'Naturally I am a little tense,' Kalila finally managed. She sat down across from her father and forced herself to take a sip of tea. 'The wedding is only in two days and—'

'You still have yet to meet your bridegroom,' Bahir finished, and there was a hard, grim note to his voice that surprised her. Of all people, she would have expected her father to understand where Zakari's duties lay. Bahir wouldn't expect a king to waste time paying court to his fiancée, not when there was royal business to attend to, diamonds to find, kingdoms to unite.

Bahir was silent, his gaze shadowed and distant. Kalila knew her father well, and she understood now that he would speak in his own time. She was content to sit in silence and watch the sun's last golden rays sink to the endless stretch of sand, painting the desert in a rainbow of vibrant yellows and oranges.

'When your mother and I arranged your marriage, Kalila,' Bahir finally said, his gaze still focused on a distant memory, 'we did so with your best interests at heart.'

'Of course, Father—'

He held up one hand, and Kalila fell silent. 'We chose Prince—King—Zakari not only because he was from a good family and heir to an important principality, but because he was young and handsome and from what we could see, a man of honour.' He turned to face her, and there was a sorrow—and regret—in his eyes that took Kalila aback. 'Kalila, we wanted the best for you, for your happiness. Of course there were other considerations. I will not pretend otherwise. There always are such things when you are a king or a queen, or a princess.' He smiled sadly. 'But your mother and I wanted your happiness. I still do.'

He fell silent, and Kalila swallowed past the painful lump of emotion in her throat. 'I know,' she whispered.

'I say this now,' Bahir continued in a brisker

voice, 'because I am concerned. I did not expect King Zakari to leave you so unattended. I hoped that perhaps you might, if not fall in love with him, then at least have some affection for him before the wedding.'

Kalila tried to smile, and almost managed it. 'That's not quite possible,' she said and Bahir frowned.

'Of course, royal duties are important, sacred. King Zakari must put his country first.' He paused, and Kalila heard—felt—the unspoken *yet*.

And yet. And yet, if Zakari had greeted her in Zaraq instead of Aarif. And yet, if he'd been here when they'd arrived. If he'd even spoken to her…

Would it have kept her from falling in love with Aarif? A few days ago, a week at most, she'd thought she *could* fall in love with Aarif. The possibility, the wonderful maybe, the hope of the uncut diamond.

Yet now that possibility had become the present, real, alive, and diamond-bright.

She loved him. It was so obvious, so overwhelming, she was amazed she hadn't realised it before. Now, gazing unseeingly at her father, she felt it resonate through her body, vibrate in her bones.

So this is what love feels like, she thought. *This is what it feels like to know why you were made, who you are.*

It felt right. It felt whole.

'Kalila?' Bahir prompted her gently. 'It is too late for regrets now, I know that well. I only speak of this now because I want you to be happy and I hope—pray—that happiness can still be found with Zakari.'

Kalila blinked; it took a moment for her father's words to penetrate. They sank into her slowly, coldly, taking away that wonderful, resonating warmth of her earlier realisation.

For a moment her love for Aarif had made her strong, happy, whole. Then truth dawned, stark and unrelenting. It didn't matter what she felt for Aarif, because she would still marry Zakari. She must, even if he didn't want to marry her.

Even if...

A new, sudden, impossible thought bloomed in her, buoyed her spirits. What if Zakari didn't want to marry her? He had professed so little interest in her so far; what if he would be grateful for a reprieve?

What if she was free?

Her father was staring at her, Kalila realised, his eyes narrowed speculatively. She forced herself to smile. 'Thank you, Father, for your words. I too hope to find happiness.' She left it at that, although she almost felt as if her father could hear her thoughts, read her heart.

Happiness that could be found only with Aarif.

She didn't see Aarif for the rest of that day, swept away as she was by preparations for the wedding. Her wedding dress, originally belonging to her mother, had to be tried on before a gaggle of appreciative women, and the resident seamstress came to make last-minute and, Kalila thought, unnecessary alterations.

She was surrounded by people now, chattering, laughing women, and after two weeks of virtual isolation she felt stifled, crowded, needing air and space. And Aarif. Every time she walked down a corridor or by a window, her gaze sought him out. She longed to see him, those dark, knowing eyes, that flickering smile, the scar that swept his cheek and reminded her of the sacrifices he'd made every day of his life, to rectify a mistake that wasn't even really his.

Aarif, however, seemed determined to keep his distance, for she didn't even catch a glimpse of him. The morning before the wedding, she was led to the palace's ancient women's quarters with its private baths for a ceremonial washing. Kalila let herself be carried along by the women's buoyant spirits and happy chattering, even though she felt as if she were separated from it all, isolated in her own bubble of apprehension and hope.

She needed to see Aarif. She needed to talk to him, explain.

She needed to tell him she loved him.

Her heart bumped against her ribs and her mouth

turned bone-dry at the thought of offering such a private revelation. She remembered his words, so callous and contemptuous, that night in the desert: *you're thinking you've fallen in love with me.*

But I have, she thought now, desperately, yet still clinging to that one shred of hope. *I have.*

The women's baths were something out of an *Arabian Nights* tale: a sunken tub the size of a small swimming pool, fragrant with rose petals and seething with foam. Kalila allowed herself to be undressed and led to the tub, allowed her hair to be washed three times with a heavy clay that felt like mud on her scalp before it was rinsed with rosewater.

The wedding was to be Western in style, so the women forewent the ceremonial hennaing of Kalila's hands and feet, slipping her instead into a white linen robe before leading her back to her room.

The heavy, cloying scents of perfumes and soap, the high-pitched giggles and provocative murmurs, the entire strangeness of it all made Kalila suddenly feel dizzy, and as they were leaving the baths she took a step back.

'Juhanah…have them go on without me. I need a moment.'

Juhanah's face softened into sympathy and she nodded. 'A moment, then, *ya daanaya*. But then you must come. This is your wedding preparation—' her voice lowered for only Kalila's ears '—even if you don't wish it.'

With her bustling sense of authority, Juhanah rounded up the other women and led them back to Kalila's rooms. Kalila sagged against the cool stone wall and closed her eyes, grateful for the silence and solitude.

I can't do this.

She opened her eyes; had she spoken aloud? She was uncomfortably aware of her still-damp skin, her pounding heart. Tomorrow she would marry Zakari; tomorrow night she would give herself to him.

The thought made bile rise in her throat and she tasted its metallic tang on her tongue.

I can't do this.

Her only hope was to talk to Aarif, yet with each hour slipping towards sunset she realised how unlikely such an opportunity would be. And then it would be too late.

Too late for her, for Aarif, for Zakari. For happiness, for hope. For love.

She swallowed and pushed herself away from the wall, her feet moving in slow, leaden steps back towards her room, and her destiny.

As she came around the latticed corner of the baths her heart seemed to leap into her throat before stopping completely for there, right in front of her, was Aarif.

* * *

Aarif stared at Kalila in both shock and hunger. His eyes roved over her figure clad only in a light robe; he could see the shadowed valley between her breasts, the flat plane of her navel—

He jerked his gaze upwards and strove for a word. A thought.

Yet what could he say? How could he excuse his presence in the women's private bathing quarters, except to admit that he had been lurking, spying like David on Bathsheba?

He'd been wandering the palace for hours, his thoughts in torment, his soul in anguish. He couldn't work; he couldn't even think. His mind— and heart—were controlled by Kalila, by images of her with him as they'd been that night in the desert—and then terrible, painful images of her with Zakari, as his bride, his queen.

She's mine.

But she wasn't, Aarif had told himself again and again. She was most certainly not his; she was forbidden, as forbidden and dangerous as Bathsheba, and he was as drawn to her as David had been.

If he were Zakari, Aarif thought with a sudden, savage bitterness, he wouldn't have let her out of his sight. If he were Zakari, he would cherish her for ever.

But he wasn't.

'Aarif…' Her voice sounded thready, and she stopped, simply staring at him as he was at her, their eyes devouring one another, as intimate and heady as a caress even though neither of them moved or touched.

Aarif opened his mouth, but not a word came out. All he could think of doing was snatching her into his arms, crushing her to him, breathing in the sweet scent of her hair, her skin—

'I'm sorry,' he finally said, his voice rasping. Her eyes widened, and he realised just how many things he had to be sorry for. 'I shouldn't be here. I thought the women had left.'

Her fingers curled around the sash of her robe as if it were a lifeline. 'Were you looking for me?'

'No.' He spoke harshly. He had to. There was no time for hope now. It was too late; it had always been too late. He swallowed down all the words he wanted to say, the professions, the promises. Pointless. 'I'm sorry,' he said again, and backed a step away.

'Aarif…' There was so much hunger and need in that voice, that one word. His name. So much striving and hope and desperation. If she spoke again, Aarif knew he would break. He would lose control, and he would take her into his arms and damn the consequences. To them all.

'I'm sorry,' he said again, and his voice broke; he heard it, felt it and knew that something inside him was breaking too, cracking apart and tearing him asunder and there was nothing he could do about it. Shaking his head, he turned and walked hurriedly away.

The moon was a pale sickle of silver in the sky when Kalila crept out of her bedroom. It was well after midnight, and the palace had settled softly into sleep.

The darkness felt like a living thing, soft and velvety, wrapping her in anonymity as she crept along the corridor. Her palms were slick and her heart was beating so loudly she felt it roaring in her ears, seeming to echo through the endless hallway as she made her way to Aarif's bedroom.

The idea had come to her that afternoon, when she'd seen a palace servant tidying a bedroom upstairs. She'd stopped the young girl and asked her where Prince Aarif's bedroom was, as she had something to return to him.

The little maid had been shocked at such a question, but Kalila was too desperate and determined to care. She'd stared her down, and finally the girl had stammered that the prince's bedroom was down the hallway, the last door on the left.

'Thank you,' Kalila said coolly, and moved away, her heart pounding, her face flushed in triumph.

All that remained was waiting…waiting through an endless dinner with a dozen faceless guests, rounds of toasts to Kalila and the still-absent Zakari, meaningless chit-chat with visiting dignitaries. She couldn't even remember what she said as she passed by one important official or royal after another, her eyes resting with the barest interest on Prince Sebastian, heir to the Aristan throne and, it would seem, Zakari's competition.

Aarif kept his distance throughout the whole meal, so she did not even meet his eyes once. She pushed the angry edge of despair this caused away, refused to acknowledge it. Tonight. She still had tonight.

It was all she had.

When the dinner was finally over, there was yet more waiting to be endured as Juhanah and the other women prepared her for bed, giggling and offering knowing smiles and sly winks that simply bounced off Kalila.

'So romantic! Like a fairy tale, Princess. You shan't see the king until your wedding day…but you know how handsome he is!'

Kalila had let the comments, the jokes and sighs, the winks and nods, wash over her. She was beyond it now. All she cared about was seeing Aarif. All she had left, her last desperate throw of the dice, was to find him and see him tonight.

She kept one hand along the wall, guiding her footsteps, as she inched her way down the dark corridor. If someone found her, what would she say? How could she explain?

Kalila could only pray that no one would.

At one point she heard low voices, masculine voices of unknown guests, and she pressed against the wall, grateful for the darkness. The men didn't come down the corridor, but moved on, to another wing of the palace. Kalila breathed a slow, silent sigh of relief.

In the darkness that one hallway seemed to go on for ever, an endless succession of doors like a circle of Dante's Inferno. She continued to inch forward until finally—finally—she came to the last door on the left. Aarif's door.

Her fingers curled slickly around the doorknob and, breathing a final prayer of supplication and hope, she turned it.

The door swung silently on its hinges; the room, Kalila saw, was swathed in darkness. The windowed doors that led to a terraced balcony were flung open to the night, and she could hear the chirring of cicadas from outside.

Her eyes, already used to the darkness, swept the room and saw within seconds that it was empty. The bed sheets were tousled, but no form lay there. The en suite bathroom, Kalila saw, was also dark.

Disappointment fell on her like a suffocating blanket, extinguishing the faint flickers of hope she'd been sustaining all afternoon, since she'd hatched this plan.

A crazy plan, a pointless one. It hadn't worked. She stood there for a moment, uncertain, not wanting to leave, unable to bear it. She could wait, she supposed, for Aarif to return, yet what if a servant came? What if he returned and he wasn't alone?

Kalila nibbled at her lower lip and as she stood there, waiting, hesitating, still hoping despite the swamping disappointment. Her choice was made for her.

'Kalila!' Aarif stood in the doorway to the balcony, and even in the darkness Kalila saw the shock, the disapproval etched on his face. Yet she was too relieved and happy to care.

'Aarif!' She stepped in the room and closed the door, leaving them both in the darkness, the moon the only light.

'What are you doing here?'

Kalila swallowed; she couldn't tear her gaze away from Aarif. He wore loose, linen trousers and no shirt; his chest was lean and brown and gloriously bare. She wanted to touch it, to feel his hot skin against hers. She craved that connection, needed that intimacy.

Aarif waited, his body tense, and Kalila swallowed and forced her gaze away from his chest. 'I needed to speak to you.'

Aarif shook his head, his arms folded. 'There is nothing to say.'

'This is our last chance to talk before I am wed,' Kalila said, trying to keep her voice level. 'Don't you think there might be something to say?'

Aarif was silent for a long moment, and then he sighed. He pulled on a shirt discarded on a chair and turned on a table lamp, bathing the room with its simple, masculine furnishings and spartan design in a warm glow. 'Very well. If you feel there is more to say, say it. Then you must go—and quickly, before your presence here is discovered.'

Kalila swallowed again. She'd hoped for a better reception than this. This was like talking to a blank face, a brick wall. How could she convince Aarif to listen? To *hear*?

How could she even know what to say?

'I've been thinking and thinking these last few days,' she began, and was ashamed to hear the telltale wobble in her voice. She lifted her chin, strengthened her spirit. 'I have to believe, Aarif, that there are more choices available to us than you're willing to consider.'

He raised one eyebrow, coldly sceptical. 'Oh?'

'Yes.' Her nails dug into her palms; she longed to wipe that cool, cynical smile off his face, strip his armour so he was as bare and vulnerable as she was. 'I realised today that Zakari has made no effort to contact me,' she said, her voice stilted, awkward. Why were the words so hard to find? 'And it made me wonder if perhaps he has as little interest in marrying me as I have in marrying him.'

She stopped, waited for Aarif to say something, for the light to dawn, the wonderful realisation.

Maybe there's a chance for us after all. But he did nothing, said nothing, just kept looking at her with that blank, bored indifference.

Kalila wanted to scream. Why was she bothering? Why was she laying herself open to this, to him, when he looked as if he couldn't wait for her to leave?

Had she been wrong?

'Maybe if we spoke to Zakari,' she forced herself to continue, 'he would realise there is no need to marry me. And…' She couldn't say it. She couldn't ask Aarif to marry her, not when he was like this. The raw humiliation was too much, too deep. 'Aarif, please,' she whispered. 'Don't look at me like that. Like you don't care, when you told me you did. I'm *trying*—' Her voice broke and she gulped back a sob, for she knew if she started to cry, she wouldn't be able to stop. She'd bawl and howl for all her disappointed dreams, and she couldn't afford that now. 'Do you love me?' she finally managed, her voice coming out in a gasp as she struggled to force the tears down, and finally succeeded.

Aarif didn't answer. A muscle beat in his jaw, and something darkened in his eyes. He was a man, Kalila realised, at war with himself, with his very nature. Duty versus desire. Honour versus love.

'Do you?' she asked again, and there was both challenge and need in her voice.

'It doesn't *matter*,' he bit out. He turned away, raking one hand through his hair in frustration. 'Kalila, don't you see? I tried to tell you before. It doesn't matter what I feel, what I want—'

'Why not?' Her voice rose in a cry, and when Aarif swung around, his look a warning, she knew just how dangerous it was for her to be here, to be heard. 'Aarif, why not?' she asked again, her voice quiet. Reasonable. 'Why don't your feelings matter? Who said they couldn't?'

'I did,' he replied flatly. 'I told you before, Kalila. My life is not my own, and it hasn't been since that day…' His throat worked, and he shook his head. 'I will not dishonour my brother by claiming for my own what is rightfully his—'

'You're talking about *me*,' Kalila interjected in a furious whisper. 'Me, a body, a human being with a heart and brain and soul. I'm not a possession—not yours, not Zakari's.'

'You agreed to this marriage—'

'Yes, and I will stand by and say my vows *if need be*. But maybe I don't need to, Aarif! Maybe Zakari would be relieved to find a way out of marriage to me, and still save the alliance between our countries. Why is it not possible? Or are you too afraid to hope, to believe that there could be something good for us? For you?'

Aarif didn't speak, he just shook his head, his

eyes stormy and dark. Kalila took a step forward, her hands held out in supplication.

'You warned me that night—the night we were as one—that I thought I was in love with you. And perhaps then I fooled myself with fairy tales, because I wanted to believe. I wanted to be rescued. But I don't want that any more, Aarif, and I know you well enough to know you aren't something out of a fairy tale and you aren't going to rescue me. I want to shape my own destiny, my own identity, and the only way I know of doing that is by loving you.'

'No—'

'Yes.' She was strong now, made strong by her love for him. 'I love you. Not like a child, or a silly girl who believes in foolish stories, but as a woman. I love the man you are, a man who believes in honour and duty and sacrifice. A man who can make me smile, and who reads silly mysteries.' Kalila was gratified to see the faintest flicker of a smile pass over Aarif like a beneficent shadow, and she continued. 'I love you, and I think you love me. Am I wrong?'

The silence was endless, mortifying. Kalila held his gaze and waited; she had nothing more to lose, and that was almost a good feeling. A strong one.

'No,' Aarif finally said, softly. 'You are not wrong.'

The rush of sweet relief made her dizzy, and she

had to reach out to grab the back of a chair to steady herself, give her the strength to continue. 'Then that's not something to take lightly, Aarif. That's not something people find every day, or even ever. And yet you're about to throw it away, without even talking to your brother—'

'Don't you realise,' Aarif cut her off, anguish tearing his voice, 'how impossible your request is? If I tell Zakari I love you, Kalila, he is put in an impossible position. It is worse than what you or I must tell him already, which is that I stole your innocence.'

'It wasn't *stealing*—'

'It was! Whether you think it or not, I was the one who should have turned away that night, I was the one who should have known to stop. But I couldn't.' There was such a hopeless despair in Aarif's voice that Kalila wanted to weep. 'God help me, I couldn't. I wanted you, I needed you, and I pushed everything else aside.' His eyes held hers with bleak honesty as he finished quietly, 'I found something in your arms I've never had anywhere else, and I shall not find it again.'

'It doesn't have to be this way—'

'Our choices have been made for us. "It is written", is it not?' He smiled, but there was no humour or happiness in the gesture, only despair. 'Kalila, take comfort if you can in knowing I love you. But you are better off with Zakari—I destroy everything I go near. At least with him you will be queen.'

'I don't want to be queen!' Her voice echoed through the room, but Kalila was too furious to care. 'I want *you*. Aarif, you cannot live your life as a punishment for what happened before. Zafir is dead, but it is not your fault—'

'Don't.' The word was quiet, lethal. Kalila knew she was treading on treacherous ground, yet this was at the heart of the matter, the poisonous root, and it had to be plucked. There was no future, no healing or happiness, until this terrible memory was made whole.

'It wasn't your fault he died,' she said quietly. 'You were responsible for him, it is true, but you didn't kidnap him. You didn't give yourself a bullet wound, you didn't do any of the things that led to his death. You must let it go.'

Aarif was silent, yet Kalila could feel the energy—the anger—pulsating from him, through the room. 'You think I don't know that?' he finally asked. 'You think I don't remind myself of it every day? Do you think my parents, my brothers and sisters, have not told me the same many times before?' His voice was pitched low, yet it throbbed with a desperate intensity. 'Do you think it *matters*?'

'It should—' Kalila whispered, and he shook his head, the motion savage.

'Do you know what I dream of? That nightmare you once rescued me from? I dream of Zafir. He is calling for me, me, not Kaliq, not anyone else. He's begging me, pleading. "Save me," he says. "Save me, Aarif."' His voice broke on his own name before he hardened his tone once more. 'He looked to me to rescue him. I hear him in my dreams, and his voice grows fainter and fainter, and then I am underwater, and I can hear nothing at all. I can do nothing. I am like a dead man.'

Kalila blinked back yet more tears. She was tired of crying, tired of being sad. She wanted happiness; she wanted it for herself and for Aarif. 'And you live life like a dead man, Aarif, waiting for your judgment. You refuse any joy, any life or love or happiness, and that is not right. No one wants that for you.' He shrugged, unmoved, and Kalila felt a sudden, clean surge of fury that even now, after so much time, so many tears, he was still implacable. Determined to mire himself in his façade of duty, live a shell of a life that no one wanted for him.

'You know what I think?' she demanded in a raw whisper. 'I think you wear your sense of duty like a shackle. Chains that bind you, keep you from trying. It's safe, isn't it? It keeps you from risking—*anything*. I think you've become so used to being numb that you're afraid to live again. To love. And that isn't the action of an honourable man. It's the action of a coward.'

Aarif's breath came out in a hiss, and Kalila

wondered if she'd gone too far. She hoped she had. It was the only way to reach him now, to pull him back into the living.

'You don't know anything about it,' Aarif snarled. 'You're willing to throw over everything you've promised simply because you want to grasp a little happiness for yourself! That, Princess, is the act of a selfish woman.'

'Maybe so,' Kalila replied steadily, 'but I told you before, I will still marry Zakari *if he wishes it*. Unlike you, Aarif, I am not willing to prostrate myself on this altar of self-sacrifice for no reason. Needless martyrdom does not appeal to me.'

He shook his head, turning away from her, cutting off the argument. Hopelessness crashed over her. Was this it, then? Her last appeal, that desperate gamble, for nothing?

The minutes ticked by in silence and finally, from a fog of despair, Kalila forced herself to speak. 'If you cannot see the sense in what I am saying, there is nothing to be done.' The words were stiff, and hardly conveyed the ache of loss that left her feeling no more than a hollow shell. 'But at least allow me what you promised, that I shall tell Zakari.' Aarif gave a jerky nod, his back still to her. 'I will tell Zakari that I am not…innocent,' Kalila continued, amazed at how steady her voice sounded. She felt ready to break apart. 'But I will not tell him that you were my lover. I'll say it was someone from university, a long time ago—'

'A lie?' Aarif interjected, whirling around, his voice incredulous and cold.

'Sometimes a lie serves better than the truth,' Kalila returned, her head held high. 'What purpose would it serve to tell Zakari about us, except perhaps to allow you to feel punished by your damnable duty?' Aarif jerked as if she'd hit him, but Kalila ploughed on. 'It certainly doesn't do him any favours, Aarif, or me, or my marriage to him. It doesn't help the stability of your family, or your country. All it does is make you feel like you've sacrificed something else, something that balances these scales that haunt you. But you'll never make up for what happened all those years ago, you will never make it right. You can only forgive yourself, and allow yourself to be forgiven by others, and you refuse to do that.'

'You don't—'

'Know?' Kalila finished. 'But I do know, and I understand you better than perhaps you want me to. I thought you loved honour, but now I wonder if it is just a shield, a mask. A way to protect yourself because it's easier. I thought you loved me, but if you really did you'd be willing to take a risk.'

'I *can't*—' Aarif burst out, and there was such trembling anguish in his voice that Kalila stilled, her self-righteous anger trickling coldly away. 'Kalila, I can't. I cannot betray my brother—my family, myself—further. And I can't believe you would love me if I did.'

'No,' Kalila said slowly, 'I wouldn't, if that's what it was. But it's not betrayal, Aarif. It's honesty.'

He shook his head, and there was such despair in that movement that Kalila's heart ached. Yet she knew she couldn't rescue him; you couldn't rescue anyone. She'd wanted to be rescued from her marriage to Zakari, but she knew now it wasn't possible. You could only forge one destiny, one identity, and that was your own.

She took a step closer to him, and then another, until they were only a whisper, a breath apart. Standing on her tiptoes, she traced his cheek, his scar, with her fingers. 'I love you,' she whispered.

Aarif made a choking sound and then, suddenly, she was gathered in his arms, and he was kissing her with a hungry intensity as if he planned to never let her go, even as they both knew it would be the last time they touched.

His hands tangled in her hair and he drew her to him, her body pressed against every intimate contour of his, and yet still he wanted to be closer, kissing her as he did with an urgency and passion that left Kalila breathless and yet wanting more.

She returned the kiss, imbued it with all the love and hope and sorrow she felt, and when it felt as if it could go on for ever she was the one who stepped away, before Aarif could thrust her from him as she knew he would make himself do.

'Goodbye,' she whispered, her voice cracking on the word, and then she fled back into the hallway and the darkness.

CHAPTER TEN

AARIF was awake to see the morning dawn. He'd been awake most of the night, until at least in the grey half-light before sunrise when he'd fallen into an uneasy sleep, and once more the old nightmare had returned.

'Aarif...Aarif...help me...'

Aarif thrashed among his twisted sheets, Zafir's voice haunting him as it always did, an endless, unfulfilled supplication.

'Aarif...'

He moaned aloud, felt himself slip under the sea, the salty water filling his mouth, his lungs—

'Aarif.'

There was no cry this time, no desperate rending of the air. Instead the voice was quiet, gentle. Forgiving. Aarif broke free from the water, climbing to the surface, and found that the sea was still. Calm.

Lying in his bed, he felt the dream recede from

his consciousness like a wave from the shore, slowly slipping away until there was nothing left but silence and peace.

Zafir was gone. He was no longer crying out, no longer pleading for help, and Aarif knew he would not hear his brother's desperate voice again.

The realisation was a blessing tinged with sorrow, and Aarif felt a sense of relief, of release. The dream was gone, and he was no longer afraid.

He opened his eyes to see the first pink finger of dawn creep across the sky, and took a deep, shuddering, healing breath.

It was finished.

Aarif swung his legs over the side of the bed and padded to the window. Outside the desert shimmered in the morning light, and the air was still fresh and cool.

Today was Kalila's wedding day. He pictured her in her bedroom, lying in her bed—had she suffered a sleepless night as he had? Had she had bad dreams?

Yet she, he knew, was responsible for the banishing of his own nightmare. He felt, for the first time in over twenty years, at peace with himself. Forgiven.

That, he thought, was Kalila's gift to him.

What would his gift to her be?

I thought you loved me, but if you really did you'd be willing to take the risk.

If he loved her. Of course he loved her; he loved

her spirit and her sense of humour, her honesty and her honour. He loved the way her eyes reflected her every thought and feeling, like a mirror to her soul. He loved her with every fibre of his being, heart, mind, body, and soul. And he knew then that Kalila was right; you couldn't throw that kind of love away.

You needed to take a risk.

Kalila awoke to the same dawn, the soft pink light streaking across the sky in pale fingers. Her body ached and her eyes felt dry and gritty; she'd barely slept at all.

As she lay in bed she heard the palace stirring to life around her: the cheerful twitter of sparrows in the garden, the whistling of a kitchen servant gone outside for an errand.

Today was her wedding day. Strange, she thought distantly, how it failed to affect her now. She felt dull, leaden, lifeless. The life had drained out of her last night, when Aarif had let her walk away.

Had she thought he wouldn't? Had she actually believed that Aarif might confront Zakari, insist on making her his bride? Kalila's mouth twisted in a grim smile. It seemed incredible now, and so it was.

Aarif didn't love her, or at least not enough. And that was all that mattered.

Although now, she supposed, it didn't matter at all; what mattered was her marriage, and the life marked out for her as Queen of Calista, King Zakari's bride.

A brisk knock sounded on the door, and before Kalila could bid someone to enter Juhanah peeked her head around.

'Good morning, Princess.'

'You're awake early,' Kalila said, trying to summon a smile and failing.

'And so are you. Today is a busy day.'

'Yes.' Kalila knew she sounded completely un-enthused, but she knew she could be honest with Juhanah. Later she would need her energy to present the charade of a loving, happy wife. Now she leaned back against the pillows and closed her eyes.

'Kalila.' Juhanah perched on the edge of the bed, one plump hand resting gently on Kalila's arm. 'You must not torture yourself like this.'

Kalila opened her eyes. 'I can't help it, Juhanah.' She lowered her voice to a whisper, conscious even now of who could be listening. 'I don't want to marry him.'

'No, and I am not surprised,' Juhanah replied with a sad little smile. 'You have not even seen him! He has not courted or wooed you, there have been no flowers, no jewels, not even a letter or message.'

Kalila shook her head, managing a wry smile. 'That wouldn't have made a difference.'

'No? You think not?' Juhanah arched one eyebrow, clearly sceptical. 'If you knew your bridegroom was eager to meet you—to *bed* you— then you would not have looked to Aarif for attention.'

'I understand what you are saying,' Kalila said quietly, wanting—needing—to be honest, 'but it wasn't like that. I never expected to fall in love with Aarif. There was very little to love about him at first, you know. But even if Zakari were here, dancing attendance on me, it would have happened.' She thought of Aarif's words: *it is written*. Perhaps it was. 'I could not have kept myself from it, Juhanah, even if I tried, which I confess I did not.'

Juhanah regarded her quietly for a moment, her lips pursed. 'Well,' she said at last, 'it is finished now. Today you will be a bride, a wife, and there is no place for Aarif.' There was a note of warning, even censure, in Juhanah's voice that made Kalila blush. What if her nurse knew the truth of that night apart? Or had she already guessed it?

'I know that, Juhanah. I doubt Aarif and I will even speak in private together again.' How would they deal with one another? she wondered. How would she survive seeing him every day, pretending he was no more than an honoured brother? How would he cope with seeing her as Zakari's wife, holding Zakari's children, when the only children she wanted were—?

Kalila let out a sudden, choked cry as the enormity of Aarif's decision last night hit her with a hammer blow. He'd exiled her for the rest of her life, forced her into a prison of unhappiness that she would never escape.

'Kalila,' Juhanah said gently, her hand tightening on Kalila's arm, 'you must let it go. Let him go. Your future is with Zakari, and by God's grace you can still love him as a wife should.'

The thought was anathema, yet Kalila knew Juhanah was right. Zakari was innocent, if negligent; she could still try to be a good wife to him. It was the only hope she had, thin thread that it was.

'Yes, you're right,' she managed at last. 'I know it, Juhanah. It's just so very hard right now.'

'Of course it is,' Juhanah soothed. 'I shall fetch your breakfast. Take a moment to compose yourself, *ya daanaya*, for the other women will be here soon and you will not be left alone all day.'

Juhanah spoke the truth, Kalila soon realised, for after breakfast her room was filled with a flurry of women, servants and siblings and guests, who were eager to help in the preparations. Kalila felt like a spectator, a ghost; she let herself be dressed, her mother's antique white gown sliding easily over her slight curves—had she lost weight? She let her hair be teased into a high cluster of shiny curls. She let her face be painted, and pearl drops fastened in her ears, a magnificent Calistan diamond necklace around her throat.

The sun was high in the sky, the palace court-yard filled with spectators and guests, luxurious black sedans and sports convertibles as everyone began to assemble for the wedding of the decade.

The wedding was in less than an hour, and Zakari still wasn't here.

Kalila choked down some lunch, although her stomach seethed with nerves. She felt awkward and stiff in her wedding gown, unused to the endless yards of pearl-encrusted satin, the veil's comb that dug into her scalp. She felt hot and un-comfortable, and almost desperately she searched for some kind of happiness or hope to carry her through the rest of the day.

'Come, they are waiting downstairs,' Juhanah said. The room had finally emptied out of people and Kalila was alone, blessedly alone. 'You must be ready.'

Kalila swallowed. It was time. Time to face her destiny, her duty. 'Is King Zakari here yet?' she asked, her voice dry and papery.

Juhanah shrugged, but then Kalila heard the answer to her question in the hectic whirring of a he-licopter above the palace. She moved to the window, and saw the helicopter with the Calistan royal insignia descend to the helipad. It was Zakari, she knew it was, and in a moment she would see him—

Then she saw another figure striding towards the landed helicopter, a figure that was familiar and beloved. Aarif. Aarif was going to meet Zakari, and suddenly Kalila knew that he was going to tell him everything. He wouldn't be able to keep from being honest, no matter what the cost to either of them.

Kalila closed her eyes, unable to bear the sight.

'Come, Princess,' Juhanah murmured, pulling her away from the window. 'There is nothing for you to see. You will see your husband as you walk down the aisle. That is as it should be.'

Kalila nodded, and let herself be led away. Her mind and body was numb, blessedly numb, as Juhanah led her through the palace corridors to a sitting room Kalila had never seen before.

'You will wait here,' Juhanah said, 'until it is time. A servant will knock on the door when it is time to go out.'

Kalila nodded. The wedding ceremony, she knew, was in the formal reception hall of the palace, an ornate room with marble pillars and a frescoed ceiling. She'd seen the servants setting up chairs there yesterday, row upon endless row.

It was tradition, borrowed from the Greeks, for the groom to hand the bride her bouquet, and distantly Kalila wondered if Zakari would remember her flowers. But of course he wouldn't have to;

someone would hand him a tasteful bouquet of roses or some such and he would give them to her with a smile as if he'd chosen them himself…

False. It was all going to be false.

The minutes ticked by in agonising slowness. Juhanah stood by the door, stout and grim-faced. Kalila was grateful that they were alone, at least; the other women had taken their seats as guests. She couldn't have borne any more chatter or gossip, winks or sly looks. It was all meant in fun, she knew, but it made her feel sick.

'What's taking so long?' she cried out in frustration after a quarter of an hour had gone by. It was past time for the ceremony to begin, and by now she just wanted it to be over.

'I don't know,' Juhanah said. She opened the door and poked her head out. 'I can't see anyone—'

'I'll go, then,' Kalila said. She felt frantic from the inactivity, the endless waiting.

'No! You cannot be seen.'

'I don't care—'

'Propriety, Kalila, is important now,' Juhanah said sharply. 'I'll go.'

Juhanah slipped out, and Kalila let out a sigh of frustration, pacing the small room like a caged animal, needing to be free.

She caught sight of her reflection in the mirror, and for a moment she stopped and stared. Her face was pale beneath the make-up, her eyes wide. Yet the dress was beautiful, her mother's gown, a dress made for a woman in love.

And I had love, Kalila realised with a pang of surprise. She knew what it was like to love and be loved, no matter for how short a time, and that was a wonderful gift. A blessing. She would cling to it for the rest of her life, knowing that Aarif had loved her.

It would have to be enough. It would be enough, she vowed, to see her through this day at least.

Juhanah returned, her eyes clouded with anxiety, her lower lip pulled between her teeth. 'I don't know what is going on,' she said in a low voice. 'There has been some delay…'

'Delay?' Kalila repeated, and heard her voice rise in fear. 'What? Why?'

Juhanah shook her head. 'I don't know. Your father—King Bahir—has been called out of the ceremony. Perhaps King Zakari wishes to discuss…'

'No.' Kalila pressed a fist to her lips. Had Aarif told, and Zakari was furious? Was she going to be shamed in front of everyone, and not just her, but Aarif too? Her heart ached for him, having already endured so much, to suffer this as well.

And yet it could provide freedom, if Zakari refused to go through with the marriage. A pointless freedom, useless without Aarif.

Just as that thought was unfurling within her a sharp knock sounded on the door, and Juhanah conversed rapidly with a servant. She turned back to Kalila, her expression resolute yet still filled with apprehension. 'It is time.'

Time. There had been so much time, and now there was none. Now it was mere minutes—seconds—before she came face to face with Zakari, without ever having spoken to him even, and pledged her life. Said her vows.

Kalila walked down the palace corridor, heard the rustle of her gown on the stone floor, felt the relentless drumming of her heart. Her hands were cold and damp and she resisted the impulse to wipe them on the sides of her gown.

Ahead of her the reception hall loomed, its wide doors thrown open, garlanded with lilies.

Kalila moved to stand on the threshold and saw a sea of faces turn expectantly to face her. Her gaze went past the rows of guests to the man standing at the end of the aisle, tall and broad-shouldered, with short, dark hair like Aarif's, his back to her.

Kalila swallowed and she felt Juhanah give her a little nudge in the small of her back. Her legs felt as if they were made of cotton wool, and her vision swam.

Think of Aarif. Think of his love.

She could do this.

She had to.

Slowly she made herself move. One foot in front of the other. The crowd had fallen to a hush, and

Kalila saw people smiling. She tried to smile back, but the smile trembled on her lips and slipped right off. She was so close to tears; she felt them at the backs of her lids, in her throat…

She swallowed them down, blinked them back, and moved on.

The aisle was endless. The papery rustling of the stiff folds of her gown was loud in her ears, loud in the expectant hush of that room. She wished Zakari would turn around, so she could see the expression on his face, except perhaps she didn't want to. Perhaps that would be worse.

Another step, and then another—she was almost there.

And then he did turn around, and Kalila nearly stumbled, the room and its hundreds of guests swimming before her eyes, for Zakari was not standing there at all.

Aarif was.

Kalila was dimly conscious of the ripple of speculative murmurs through the crowd, but it was nothing compared to the shock vibrating through her whole being. She stood there, rooted to the spot, her mind unable to catch up, wondering if it was some kind of trick…

Aarif was close enough to touch, and he reached out and curled his hand around her elbow, steadying her, bringing her closer.

When she was close enough so that she alone

could hear him speak, he whispered, 'Do you still want me?'

Kalila stared at him, saw the need and hope and love in his eyes, and could only nod. The tears were close again.

'Kalila?' Aarif demanded, his voice still pitched low, and she knew what he needed to hear.

'I love you.'

He smiled then, and Kalila saw the sheen of tears in his own eyes. 'And I love you. More than life.'

Aarif handed her a bouquet of flowers, and Kalila's fingers closed around it automatically. She looked down and saw the delicate, curling petals of a bouquet of irises. Her favourite, just as she'd told Aarif. He'd remembered.

Someone cleared his throat, and Kalila realised there was a man standing next to Aarif, also tall and broad-shouldered, smiling faintly. Zakari.

She smiled back, feeling strange, light-headed, and yet absurdly, wonderfully happy, and the ceremony began.

Kalila was barely conscious of the words being spoken, the vows being said. Her mind was still thrumming with awareness of Aarif, the realisation that she was actually marrying him.

It wasn't until the ceremony was over, and they were walking back down the aisle, that she realised this was real. *He* was real.

Out in the corridor, she turned to him, breathless. 'Tell me—'

'Later.' Aarif pulled her into his arms and kissed her, a kiss that had no secrecy or danger or shame, only love, as pure and brilliant as the finest diamond.

Kalila surrendered herself to the kiss, to the love that flowed between them and through her veins, bubbling up into wondrous joy.

Finally she pulled away, laughing, her hair starting to come undone from its artful cluster in curly tendrils. 'Tell me,' she commanded, 'how you came to be standing there instead of your brother.'

Light danced in Aarif's eyes. 'Are you glad?'

'You know I am!'

Aarif laughed, and it was a sound Kalila loved to hear. She hadn't heard it many times before, and certainly not with such joyous unrestraint.

Aarif pulled her away from the guests pouring out of the reception hall, into a quiet antechamber.

His face had turned serious again, his eyes dark. 'Last night I couldn't sleep. All I could do was think of everything you'd said to me, every accusation and judgment, and realise they were all true.'

'Aarif—' Kalila began, but he held up a hand to stop her.

'Wait. Let me say this, for God knows I should have said it yesterday, and spared us both a sleepless night.' He smiled wryly before his expression sobered once more. 'Kalila, you told me I was trying to balance the scales, and though I'd never thought of that before I realised you were right. That's exactly what I was doing. For the last twenty-one years I've been trying to atone for Zafir's death, even though no one expected me to. It was something I expected of myself, even though I doomed myself to failure from the start. And happiness—love—they were things I didn't even dare dream of.' He shook his head. 'But it's amazing how a prison can become safe. Comfortable, even. And the more I withdrew from life, the less appealing the kinds of risks and dangers living create became to me…all without me even realising it. All I could see was that in loving you, I'd betrayed Zakari. And that night we had together—as right as it felt to have you in my arms—was a betrayal, of a kind. But I realised last night that to allow your marriage to Zakari to go forward without even a word of protest was another betrayal. A betrayal of you, and myself, and what we have shared.'

Kalila thought of Aarif striding so resolutely towards the helicopter. 'So what did you tell Zakari?'

'I told him what happened between us, and that I loved you. I asked for his forgiveness and said that I wanted to marry you.'

'He must have been surprised,' Kalila said

weakly, unable to even imagine such a conversation.

'He was, but he was also happy…for me.' Aarif shook his head in wonder. 'My brother is a good man.' He paused, his expression becoming shadowed. 'I told him if he still wished to marry you, I would be forced to stand aside. I do not think you would love me if I had not said that.'

'I know,' Kalila whispered, her throat aching with unshed tears. 'I feel the same.'

'But I also told him that we loved each other, and I would do everything in my power to make you happy and bring honour to both Calista and Zaraq.'

'And what did he say?' Kalila could not even imagine the king's reaction.

Aarif smiled wryly. 'He was shocked, to be sure. But then he laughed, and told me he could tell that I loved you, for he'd never seen me so happy before, and who was he to stand in the way of such love.'

Kalila shook her head in amazement. 'He is indeed a good man.'

'Yes, he is,' Aarif agreed. 'And so is your father. Zakari called him out of the ceremony to explain the situation, and he didn't even look flustered, or very surprised. He graciously agreed, saying that the alliance between our countries would still stand.'

'He told me he wanted my happiness.'

'And does he have it?' Aarif asked. He brought her hand to his lips, kissing her fingers. 'You're happy with this slow-witted husband of yours, who wasn't able to understand his own nature until his wife told him?'

'Very happy,' Kalila whispered, and Aarif kissed her again.

A knock sounded on the door, and Kalila heard a rueful voice exclaim, 'Enough already! The reception—and all your guests—are waiting!'

Laughing, Aarif led her from the chamber to another of the palace's great halls, where guests circulated amidst servants bearing trays of champagne.

As they entered the room a spontaneous round of applause burst forth, and Kalila flushed in both embarrassment and pride. Granted, she thought, it was a bit unusual to have a change of grooms on the day of the wedding, but she was too happy to care if anyone was shocked, and from the looks on people's faces they only wished her and Aarif every joy.

After a round of toasts, Zakari approached them, smiling wryly. 'May I offer my felicitations to the bride?' he said, sketching a slight bow before them.

'Yes, of course, thank you,' Kalila murmured. She glanced up at him, saw that he was as handsome and charming as she'd remembered as a girl, and yet he wasn't Aarif.

'Kalila, you must be an extraordinary woman indeed to have brought my brother to his senses at last. I have never seen him so carefree, so happy.'

'She is extraordinary,' Aarif murmured, his arm around Kalila's waist, drawing her close. 'I am most blessed.'

'I hope one day to be similarly blessed,' Zakari said, and then added with a devilish grin, 'although not today it seems. Brother, a moment of your time before you retire with your bride?' Zakari raised his eyebrows, and with a little nod of assent Kalila watched them draw aside.

'I meant what I said,' Zakari said in a low voice, his hand heavy on Aarif's shoulder. 'I am happy for you both, and I wish you every blessing.'

'Thank you,' Aarif said, his own voice choked, for his brother's blessing made his cup wondrously overflow. 'You are a good man, Zakari.'

'And so are you, brother,' Zakari returned, 'though you have not always thought you are.' Aarif nodded, and found himself overcome with emotion. He was grateful when Zakari switched the conversation to business.

'It is just as well things have happened as they did, for I must leave again tonight. I have heard a rumour that King Aegeus had an affair with a palace maid—years ago, you understand, but there might be something in it.'

'A clue to the missing diamond?' Aarif asked, and Zakari nodded.

'Yes.' Zakari's voice hardened. 'I will find that

diamond, Aarif. No matter what happens.' Aarif nodded. He'd never understood the driving determination his brother had to find the diamond, yet he accepted it. Everyone had their own memories, shadows, and ghosts.

Yet thanks to Kalila, his had been released. 'God be with you in your journey.' He clapped his brother's shoulder and Zakari returned the gesture.

'Now you should steal your bride away while there is time. Otherwise you'll be carousing with your guests all evening, and that is no way to spend a wedding night.'

'No indeed.' Aarif grinned, and, taking leave of his brother, he turned back to Kalila.

Kalila suddenly found her mouth was dry, her mind uncertain. She wanted nothing more than to be alone with Aarif, yet now that the moment had come she found herself strangely nervous.

'Come,' Aarif murmured, and he drew her away from the crowd. He led her upstairs, not to his bedroom, but to another room, in its own wing, separate from the rest of the palace.

'Consider this the Calistan honeymoon suite,' he said as he threw open the door. Kalila stepped inside, her surprised gaze taking in the huge bedroom with its lavish four-poster bed piled high with pillows, the wide windows thrown open to the night. Someone had come before them and lit candles, so the room was full of soft, flickering shadows. She saw champagne chilling in a bucket, two fluted glasses waiting to be filled.

It was, she thought, like something out of a fantasy or a fairy tale, something she would have dreamed as a girl.

Yet it was real. The fairy tale was real.

'This is a bit different from a tent in the desert,' she managed, and Aarif smiled, drawing her to him.

'Yes…and I'm not sure which I prefer.'

'This is more comfortable at least,' Kalila joked, and Aarif touched his finger to her chin, tilting her head so she met his eyes.

'*Ayni*, are you afraid?' he asked.

'Not afraid,' Kalila said a bit shakily. 'Just…uncertain. It's hard to believe this is real. That it's…*all right*.'

Aarif laughed softly. 'It is a miracle, is it not? There is no shame here, no secrecy or fear. There is only you and me…and our love.'

He drew her into his arms, his kiss soft yet filled with promise, and Kalila felt her fears melt away. Aarif loved her, and she loved him; it *was* real. Not a fairy tale, but something much better.

She had found herself in love; they had found each other. Smiling, the candlelight creating dancing shadows around them, she reached for Aarif and led him to their marriage bed.

THE ROYAL
HOUSE OF KAREDES

Two crowns, two islands, one legacy

**A royal family, torn apart by pride and its lust
for power, reunited by purity and passion**

The islands of Adamas have been torn into
two rival kingdoms:

TWO CROWNS
The Stefani diamond has been split as a
symbol of their feud

TWO ISLANDS
Gorgeous Greek princes reign supreme
over glamorous Aristo
Smouldering sheikhs rule the desert island of Calista

ONE LEGACY
Whoever reunites the diamonds will rule all.

Turn the page to discover more!

THE KINGDOM OF ADAMAS:
A TURBULENT HISTORY

The islands of Calista and Aristo have always been a temptation to world powers. Initially this was because of their excellent positions for trading and the agricultural potential of Aristo's luscious, fertile land. The discovery of diamonds on Calista in the Middle Ages made the kingdom a target for invaders.

The kingdom passed through the hands of many foreign powers throughout the ages. Originally part of the Ancient Greek Empire, Adamas then came under the control of Rome from 150 BC onwards. Following the fall of the Roman Empire approximately four hundred years later, the islands were annexed to Byzantine control.

It was not until Richard the Lionheart seized Adamas in the twelfth century that the family of Karedes, local island nobility, was installed on the throne. When the republic of Venice briefly took control in the fifteenth century the Karedes dynasty continued to rule as mere figureheads.

Thereafter followed a period of struggle for the royal family. The Ottoman Empire claimed the islands in the sixteenth century and they were forced into an exile that lasted nearly two hundred years. When the Turks finally sold the islands to the British in 1750 the royal family was finally reinstated but the kingdom did not gain its independence until 1921.

The death of King Christos in 1974 marked the end of the kingdom of Adamas. The islands have functioned under separate rule ever since.

THE STEFANI DIAMOND

Diamonds have been prized since the dawn of human history for their unique qualities. The jewels were first discovered in India in 800 BC, and brought to Europe by Alexander the Great five hundred years later.

In 1477, Mary of Burgundy became the first known recipient of a diamond engagement ring given to her by the Archduke Maximilian of Austria. This begins the history and tradition of diamond engagement rings.

The Koh-i-Noor and the Hope diamonds were brought to Europe in 1631. In 1792, the Hope Diamond was stolen from the French crown jewels during the French Revolution. In 1851, The Koh-i-Noor diamond was re-cut to one hundred and five carats for Queen Victoria (Empress of India). This famous diamond is part of the British Crown jewels.

In the medieval period, a beautiful pink diamond was discovered on Calista, and used in the Karedes crown to symbolise the power of the Karedes's rule. The jewel became known as the Stefani (meaning: Crown) diamond. It quickly took on a deeply symbolic role in the kingdom of Adamas. Believing that their power resided in the stone, the Karedes family vowed that it would never leave their hands. If the jewel was lost, their kingdom would fall. The existence of this diamond fuelled treasure-hunters' dreams for centuries, but no other diamond of any size was found on Calista until the 1940s.

In 1972, faced with increasing tension from his kingdom, the islands of Aristo and Calista and with family pressure, King Christos announced that after his death the two islands would split. In the presence of his children Anya and Aegeus, witnessed by the court, Christos declared:

"You will rule each island for the good of the people, and bring out the best in your kingdom, but my wish is that eventually these two jewels, like the islands, will be reunited. Aristo and Calista are more successful, more beautiful and more powerful as one nation, Adamas."

After King Christos died in 1974, the one Stefani diamond was split into two, to form two stones for the coronation crowns of Aristo and Calista and fulfil the ancient charter.

THE TOURIST'S GUIDE TO ARISTO AND CALISTA

The island of Aristo

The island's name itself means best – and it certainly lives up to that as a holiday destination! The sunny climate and beautiful coastline have made it a favourite destination for jet-set holidaymakers. It is an incredibly rich principality, a world-renowned financial centre and provides tranquil luxury and a decadent party scene, complete with fabulous restaurants and nightclubs, a golf course, a marina and a casino.

Things to see

Don't miss the impressive Royal Palace in the centre of the island, just inland from the bay of Apollonia. The beautiful old quarter and port of Messaria are well worth a visit – especially to spend your casino winnings in fabulous boutiques! Long white sandy beaches on the north-east coast are banked by fertile plains. A number of fabulous tourist resorts are dotted along the north-east coast where the rich and famous can relax in five-star hotels and spas, or in gated mansions with infinity pools, private tennis courts and landscaped gardens. If your taste is more for city life, enjoy the ultra-modern city, Ellos, where high-rise corporations reach for the sky.

Things to do

Ellos is packed with exclusive bars, restaurants and spas and is famous for its glittering nightlife. The Grand Hotel is the centre of Ellos's nightlife – don't miss your chance to spot celebrities in its fabulous restaurant!

The island of Calista

Calista (meaning: beautiful one) is the destination of choice for more laid-back tourism. The sleepy island is an unspoiled paradise with an understated tourism industry. In contrast to neighbouring island Aristo, Calista has a hot, dry climate and arid terrain. The central portion of the island is entirely desert and inhabitants reside on the more hospitable north-facing coast. As its agricultural prospects have never been great, the island has retained its stunning natural beauty. Famous for the wealth of diamonds below the surface of the rock, the main river Kordela is also source of glittering diamond deposits.

Things to see

Modern Calista has an intact historical centre called Serapolis which is still the beating heart of the city. It retains a strong middle-eastern influence both culturally and architecturally and noisy, colourful markets fill the labyrinth of winding streets. Don't miss the beautiful Royal Palace.

Things to do

You'll pick up bargains and enjoy some delicious street food in the marketplace of Serapolis. Explore the Azahar desert – on the back of a camel for the intrepid – and spend a night in an oasis. Walk the diamond fields and try to find your own glittering stone as a souvenir of your stay in this peaceful place. For an injection of glamour and luxury, visit the new town and resort of Jaladhar.

LETTERS FROM
THE HOUSE OF KAREDES

A hastily scribbled note to Andonis, grounds keeper at the Royal Palace, from Princess Anya:

Andonis,

It is all over. I have lost our baby because of Aegeus. My brother discovered our affair and he was angry – so angry that he hit me. I fell and now our child is gone, Andonis. I cannot bear it. My brother has ruined everything. I will never forgive Aegeus for the hurt that he has caused, but our love is cursed. We cannot be together.

Anya

Aegeus to Lydia, his maid, in 1974 on the death of his father:

Dearest Lydia,

Love, you must put me from your mind. Forced by duty and by circumstance, I must go through with my betrothal. Tia deserves better than this, but my family and my loyalty demand this farce of a wedding.

It would be better if you were to go to Calista for now. I don't trust myself to remain near you and remember my duty. We must part. But come to me in Aristo every year on the anniversary of our wedding. It is not enough. It will never be enough. Wear the diamond for me.

I know you will understand, my beautiful Lydia. It is a son's duty and the king's command.

Yours eternally,

Aegeus

KATE HEWITT

discovered her first Mills & Boon® romance on a trip to England when she was thirteen, and she's continued to read them ever since.

She wrote her first story at the age of five, simply because her older brother had written one and she thought she could do it too. That story was one sentence long – fortunately, they've become a bit more detailed as she's grown older.

She has written plays, short stories, and magazine serials for many years, but writing romance remains her first love. Besides writing, she enjoys reading, travelling, and learning to knit.

After marrying the man of her dreams – her older brother's childhood friend – she lived in England for six years and now resides in Connecticut with her husband, her three young children, and the possibility of one day getting a dog.

Kate loves to hear from readers – you can contact her through her website, www.kate-hewitt.com.

Read on for our exclusive interview with Kate Hewitt!

We chatted to Kate Hewitt about the world of
THE ROYAL HOUSE OF KAREDES. Here are
her insights!

Would you prefer to live on Aristo or Calista? What appeals to you most about either island?

Definitely Calista! I like the exotic remoteness of it, without too much of the glitz.

What did you enjoy about writing about The Royal House of Karedes?

I really enjoyed exploring the ready-made world of Calista and the royal family, while still being able to flesh the story out for myself. The best of both worlds!

How did you find writing as part of a continuity?

It was tricky at first, because you had to consider everyone else's stories, but I really got into it and had a great time.

When you are writing, what is your typical day?

My children are all in school for the first time so I am now trying to write three or so hours every morning, as opposed to at night, which is what I did before. I usually find my time disappears, however, with errands and chores and so forth, so I end up writing at night too.

Where do you get your inspiration for the characters that you write?

From the depths of my subconscious, which is fed by all the people I see (living in New York City, there is plenty of opportunity for people-watching!).

What did you like most about your hero and heroine in this continuity?

I liked how star-crossed my lovers were – their situation seemed truly hopeless, and yet love prevailed – of course!

What would be the best – and worst – things about being part of a royal dynasty?

The wealth and luxury would be the best; having to conform to expected standards and being watched all the time the worst. I like being a commoner!

Are diamonds really a girl's best friend?

Only if you want to be lonely.

*Who will reunite the Stefani Diamond
and rule Adamas?*

Don't miss the next book in the fabulous
ROYAL HOUSE OF KAREDES:

THE GREEK BILLIONAIRE'S
INNOCENT PRINCESS

BY CHANTELLE SHAW

Plain, plump – and pregnant!

Plain, plump Kitty Karedes is the forgotten princess
– until she has to host the palace ball. Kitty plans
everything perfectly, forgetting only to buy herself a
show-stopping dress!

At the ball, Greek shipping tycoon Nikos Angelaki
mistakes homely Kitty for a waitress. She flees, her
confidence in tatters but her identity still a secret.
When Nikos spies her again, she's swimming naked
in the moonlight and he realises her frumpy clothes
were hiding luscious curves! But next morning Nik
discovers he's seduced a princess – and he's made her
pregnant with his baby!

Turn the page for
an exclusive extract!

Nikos Angelaki stood at the edge of the ballroom and surveyed the five hundred or so guests who were dancing or sipping champagne beneath the ornate chandeliers. The men were uniform in black tuxedos, while the women – dressed in couture gowns and flaunting a spectacular array of diamonds and precious gems – flitted about the dance floor like gaudy butterflies. He flicked back the cuff of his dinner jacket, glanced at his Rolex, and then began to make his way across the room – aware of the interested glances he received as he passed. At thirty-two he was used to the attention his looks and the rumours of his wealth attracted. An attractive blonde in a daringly low-cut dress caught his attention, and his gaze lingered on her fleetingly before he stepped into the lobby.

It was the first time he had attended the royal ball or visited the Aristan Palace, and he was impressed by the elegant splendour of the rooms where the silk-covered walls were lined with priceless works of art. The ruling family of the House of Karedes were one of the wealthiest families in Europe, and the guest list included members of the aristocracy and heads of state – grand people who had no idea that the Prince Regent's honoured guest tonight had grown up in the slums of Athens.

Nikos wondered cynically if the butler who had escorted him to the state drawing room to greet Prince Sebastian would have been quite so obsequious if he'd known that Nikos's mother had once worked as a lowly kitchen maid at the palace. However, that was something he hadn't even revealed to Sebastian, despite the close friendship that had developed between them.

He strode across the hall, pushed open a door, and found himself in the banqueting suite, which was empty, apart from a waitress at the far end of the room who – unlike the other palace staff who seemed to be rushed off their feet tonight – was idly folding napkins.

The guests had eaten earlier, but Nikos's delayed flight had meant that he had missed the buffet supper, and as he glanced at the mouth-watering selection of canapés he was aware of a hollow feeling in his stomach. Business first, he told himself firmly. It was evening in Aristo, but early afternoon on America's east coast and he had arranged to call a client in New York. He strolled towards the waitress who had her back to him and was still oblivious to his presence.

"Can you tell me if there is somewhere I can be uninterrupted? I need to make an urgent business call."

The deep, gravelly voice was so innately sensual that the tiny hairs on Kitty's body stood on end, and she turned her head, her heart crashing in her chest when she stared up at the man who had come silently into the room. She had recognised him instantly when he had walked into the ballroom earlier in the evening – Nikos Angelaki, billionaire shipping magnate, notorious playboy, and in recent months one of her brother's closest confidants. Sebastian had explained that he had met Nikos at a business function in Greece, and since then the two men had discovered a mutual liking for poker and the roulette wheel in the nightclubs of Aristo and Athens.

The photographs Kitty had seen of him in the tabloids had triggered her interest, but nothing had prepared her for the impact of Nikos in the flesh. He was suave, sophisticated and spine-tinglingly sexy. Taller than average; his tapered black trousers emphasised his long legs and taut thighs, while his impeccably tailored dinner jacket cloaked formidably broad shoulders. But it was his face that captured her attention. Handsome was a barely adequate description of the chiselled perfection of his features; the slanting, razor-sharp cheekbones and square chin, the heavy brows arched above midnight dark eyes, and a wide, sensual mouth.

In the silence that stretched between them Kitty sensed his arrogance and devil-may-care confidence, and she felt an unbidden and shockingly intense tug of sexual awareness that sent a quiver down her spine. He was gorgeous, but she suddenly realised that she was staring at him, and she blushed.

THE ROYAL HOUSE OF KAREDES

Two crowns, two islands, one legacy

Volume Five
THE GREEK BILLIONAIRE'S INNOCENT PRINCESS
by Chantelle Shaw

Plain, plump – and pregnant!

At the palace ball, Greek shipping tycoon Nikos Angelaki mistakes plain, plump Kitty Karedes for a waitress. When Nikos spies her again, she's swimming naked in the moonlight and he realises her frumpy clothes were hiding luscious curves!

But next morning Nik discovers he's seduced a princess – and he's made her pregnant with his baby!

Available 21st August 2009

www.millsandboon.co.uk   M&B

THE ROYAL HOUSE OF KAREDES

Two crowns, two islands, one legacy

Volume 1 – April 2009
BILLIONAIRE PRINCE, PREGNANT MISTRESS
by Sandra Marton

Volume 2 – May 2009
THE SHEIKH'S VIRGIN STABLE-GIRL
by Sharon Kendrick

Volume 3 – June 2009
THE PRINCE'S CAPTIVE WIFE
by Marion Lennox

Volume 4 – July 2009
THE SHEIKH'S FORBIDDEN VIRGIN
by Kate Hewitt

8 VOLUMES IN ALL TO COLLECT!

THE ROYAL HOUSE OF KAREDES

Two crowns, two islands, one legacy

Volume 5 – August 2009
THE GREEK BILLIONAIRE'S INNOCENT PRINCESS
by Chantelle Shaw

Volume 6 – September 2009
THE FUTURE KING'S LOVE-CHILD
by Melanie Milburne

Volume 7 – October 2009
RUTHLESS BOSS, ROYAL MISTRESS
by Natalie Anderson

Volume 8 – November 2009
THE DESERT KING'S HOUSEKEEPER BRIDE
by Carol Marinelli

8 VOLUMES IN ALL TO COLLECT!

MILLS & BOON®
MODERN™

...International affairs, seduction and passion guaranteed

The Greek Tycoon's Pregnant Wife
Anne Mather

Miranda Lee
Blackmailed into the Italian's Bed

MILLS & BOON
MODERN™

MILLS & BOON
MODERN™

8 brand-new titles each month

Available on the first Friday of every month
from WHSmith, ASDA, Tesco
and all good bookshops
www.millsandboon.co.uk

GEN/01/RTL11

MILLS & BOON

MODERN *Heat*

If you like Mills & Boon Modern you'll love Modern Heat!

Strong, sexy alpha heroes, sizzling storylines and exotic locations from around the world – what more could you want!

2 brand-new titles each month

Available on the first Friday of every month
from WHSmith, ASDA, Tesco
and all good bookshops
www.millsandboon.co.uk

GEN/06/RTL11

GEN/14/RTL12

MILLS & BOON®

Blaze

Scorching hot sexy reads...

1 2-in-1 and 2 single brand-new titles each month

Available on the first Friday of every month
from WHSmith, ASDA, Tesco
and all good bookshops
www.millsandboon.co.uk

MILLS & BOON®
Desire™ 2-in-1

2 passionate, dramatic love stories in each book

3 brand-new titles to choose from each month

Available on the third Friday of every month
from WHSmith, ASDA, Tesco
and all good bookshops
www.millsandboon.co.uk

GEN/51/RTL11